SOMETHING WAS TERRIBLY WRONG

The threesome stopped outside the entrance to the ornate stone tomb. There stood Perry's statue, smiling weirdly at them and pointing toward the door. But the wrought-iron gates had once again been wrenched open, and on the broad marble steps lay an open coffin. The lid lay nearby, and it was cracked and splintered, as if someone had forced it loose with a crowbar.

"Heavenly days, McGee!" the professor whispered in an awestruck tone. "It looks as if a ghoul has been wandering around. I cannot imagine . . ." His voice trailed off as he bent over the empty coffin and touched the quilted lining with his fingers. Then, with a haunted look in his eyes, he turned back to the boys. "I'm afraid that mischief is afoot," he announced solemnly. "Mischief and dirty dealing and the Lord knows what. Who on earth would be so rotten as to steal my poor brother's corpse? *Who?*"

THE CHESSMEN
OF DOOM

JOHN BELLAIRS

Frontispiece
by Edward Gorey

A BANTAM SKYLARK BOOK®
NEW YORK · TORONTO · LONDON · SYDNEY · AUCKLAND

RL 5, age 10 and up

*This edition contains the complete text
of the original hardcover edition.*
NOT ONE WORD HAS BEEN OMITTED.

THE CHESSMEN OF DOOM

*A Bantam Skylark Book / published by arrangement with
Dial Books for Young Readers*

PRINTING HISTORY
Dial Books edition published 1989
Bantam edition / May 1991

*Skylark Books is a registered trademark of Bantam Books,
a division of Bantam Doubleday Dell Publishing Group, Inc.
Registered in U.S. Patent and Trademark Office and elsewhere.*

*Bantam Books are published by Bantam Books, a division of Bantam
Doubleday Dell Publishing Group, Inc. Its trademark, consisting of the
words "Bantam Books" and the portrayal of a rooster, is Registered in U.S.
Patent and Trademark Office and in other countries. Marca Registrada.
Bantam Books, 666 Fifth Avenue, New York, New York 10103.*

PRINTED IN THE UNITED STATES OF AMERICA

CWO   0 9 8 7 6 5 4 3

The Chessmen
of Doom

CHAPTER ONE

"Yes, my name is Childermass. And you are standing in my nasturtium bed. Kindly get your fat feet out of it, at once!"

It was a sunny mild May afternoon in the mid–1950's. Professor Roderick Childermass was sitting in a dirty yellow-and-green-striped lawn chair in the yard behind his house, and he was glaring at a young man who stood in an oblong bed of earth near the back porch. Professor Childermass was short, elderly, and cranky-looking. His nose was red and pitted, and his hair was white and unruly. Overgrown sideburns sprouted from both sides of his face, and his eyes glittered behind gold-rimmed spectacles. The young man wore the gray uniform of a post office employee, and in one hand he clutched a letter with a red-white-and-blue-striped sticker on it. With a sudden motion the postman extricated himself from the flower bed and held out the letter for the professor to take.

"Sorry, sir," he said apologetically. "I have a special-delivery letter here for you."

With a sigh the professor put down the glass of lemonade, heaved himself up out of the chair, and snatched the letter from the young man. "Special delivery, is it!" muttered the professor under his breath. "Hmm . . . well, thank you very much. Run along now." He made a shooing motion with his hand.

The young man muttered. Then he turned and left. The professor stuck his thumb under a corner of the envelope's flap and ripped. He pulled out the folded letter and shook it open with a single quick snap of his wrist. Then he began to read:

My dear Roderick:

Greetings! By the time you get this, I will be in the next world, if there is one. My body will be in its tomb, or green and festering in its shroud, as Shakespeare would say. But let's not dwell on unpleasant details: I'm dead, and I've left my estate in Maine to you. There are conditions that must be fulfilled, but then you've guessed that by now, haven't you, you clever old cuss? In a few days a lawyer will be calling you to tell what you have to do to inherit my ten million smackeroos. In the meantime, in between time, let me just leave you with this thought:

Why a dead eye in a room with no view?
Why pallid dwarves on a board that's not true?
To pull the hairy stars from their nest
And give sinful humans a well-deserved test.

If you solve this riddle you may wish that you hadn't. Hard times are ahead for the cruel and heartless Lords of War.

Yours ever,
Peregrine P. Childermass

The professor sat staring at this odd letter for a long time. He hated mysterious notes, and the longer he thought about this one, the madder he got. Of course, he was sorry that Peregrine was dead, but he was also angry at his brother because Peregrine had decided to play some kind of insane trick on him. "Peregrine, if you were here and alive, I'd belt you one in the snoot! he muttered, as he sipped lemonade and tried to calm down. The professor did not mind the idea of inheriting ten million bucks, but he wondered what "conditions" his batty brother had in mind in order for him to get the money. As for the little poem that had come with the letter, he did not have the faintest idea of what it meant. Nothing, probably.

A few days later the professor was across the street having Sunday dinner with his friends the Dixons and their grandson, Johnny. The Dixons were an elderly couple who had lived in Duston Heights, Massachusetts, for many years. One day their grandson John had come to live with them, because his mother was dead and his dad was fighting in the Korean War. Johnny was a short blond boy who wore glasses. He was brainy and shy and had trouble getting people to like him. Strangely enough he got along fine with cranky old Professor Childermass, who terrified most people. The two of them had become friends a few seconds after they met, and now the old man was like a second father to Johnny. They played chess and baked cakes and discussed the problems of the world together. It was an odd friendship, but it worked.

At the Dixons' the professor rambled on about the letter he had gotten. He stuffed mashed potatoes and roast beef into his mouth and went on and on about his brother Peregrine and the rest of his nutty family. The professor's father had taught literature at Princeton, and he had named his sons for characters in the novels of Tobias Smollett. There was Roderick Random, and Peregrine Pickle, and Humphrey Clinker, and even Ferdinand Count Fathom, who usually signed his name F. C. F. Childermass. All of the Childermass boys had turned out to be pretty strange—except, of course, for the professor himself. He was perfectly normal—at least, he said so.

As the professor rattled on, Johnny kept thinking about

the four-line poem and the words at the end of the letter about the heartless Lords of War.

"Professor," he said suddenly, when the old man had paused to take a drink of water, "who are the Lords of War? Is he talking about people who make guns and bombs?"

The professor shrugged. "I suppose so," he muttered, "though I really can't be sure what anything in that blasted letter means. Peregrine claims that the Lords of War are in for hard times. Maybe he read the tea leaves in the bottom of his cup and decided that an era of peace was coming to the world. Peregrine was one of those people who get very upset about the horrors of war, and he always said that there ought to be some way to frighten human beings into being peaceful. That's a nice notion, isn't it? But not very practical. Someday the earth may be peaceful, but unless an angel with a flaming sword appears in the sky, I don't see how it's going to happen."

Grampa Dixon was sitting at the head of the table. He was a tall, gaunt old man with saggy cheeks and gold-rimmed spectacles. Grampa was kindly and timid and he usually kept silent when the professor was ranting on about something. Finally, however, he spoke up.

"Rod," he asked suddenly, "are you gonna take Perry's money if they offer it to ya?"

The professor rolled his eyes toward the ceiling. "It all depends," he said, "on what the conditions of his will are. If they ask me to sacrifice kittens on the altar of Baal, I probably won't take it. But if I have to put on a pink nightgown and run around town at midnight shouting, *The British are coming!* then I'll do it. We'll just have to see."

Later that evening Johnny was sitting in the professor's kitchen watching as the old man frosted a chocolate layer cake. The professor smeared dollop after dollop of rich fudge frosting. When the cake was done they were going to gorge on it, something they both very much enjoyed. But just as the professor was adding some more powdered sugar to the frosting in his mixing bowl, the phone rang. With the spatula in his hand he went over to the sideboard and picked up the receiver. The conversation that followed was punctuated by lots of "ums" and "ers" from the professor, but somehow Johnny figured out that the caller was somebody who had something to do with the late Peregrine Childermass's will. With a half-smothered curse the professor said good-bye and hung up. He turned to Johnny and sighed wearily.

"That was Perry's lawyer," he muttered, as he went back to the business of frosting the cake. "He told me the terms of Perry's idiotic will. It seems that I have to spend the summer—from June fifteenth till Labor Day—at Perry's run-down estate and I have to cut the grass and whip the place into shape without any hired help. Ah, well! I suppose it won't kill me. Maybe it'll keep me from getting all flabby and pale-faced this summer."

"You mean you're gonna go?" asked Johnny eagerly.

The professor frowned and dipped his finger into the frosting. Slowly he lapped up the fudgy goo. "I'm not sure," he muttered. "Peregrine's lawyer is sending the papers to my lawyer, and then I can read all the small print. We shall see."

Several days passed, and during that time Johnny did not see the professor much. One afternoon when he was walking on Merrimack Street, the main street of the town, he saw the professor coming out of the law offices of McKillop and Ward. Johnny waved to him and the professor turned and smiled wearily.

"Greetings, John!" he said. "I have just been wading through unimaginable acres of legal nincompoopery, and I'm ready to go home and take a sleeping potion that will knock me out for three or four days. *Aargh!* Can't legal forms *ever* be simple? Why, I remember once when . . ."

On and on the professor rambled. Johnny was used to the old man's tirades, so he just walked beside him with an amused smile on his face. Finally, when the professor paused to catch his breath, Johnny spoke up.

"Professor," he asked, timidly, "are you gonna go up to your brother's place to stay this summer?"

The professor threw a quick, nervous look at Johnny. Then he smiled and nodded. "Yes, I suppose that I will. I have some misgivings about the whole business—fears, I suppose. I can't put it into words, but that wacky poem of Perry's has been on my mind night and day since I got his letter, and I can't help feeling that there is something sinister about it. But then, I've always been a worrier—I expect the worst things to happen, and when they don't I'm always surprised. Nevertheless, I would be crazy to turn down ten million clams because of groundless fears. Right?"

Johnny said nothing—he just shrugged. They had reached the professor's car. But before they got in, the old man laid a hand on his friend's shoulder.

"John," the professor asked, "do you suppose . . . that is, would you and Byron like to come up with me on this trip? It might be fun for the two of you."

CHAPTER TWO

Johnny was startled by this suggestion. School would be out soon, and he thought he would be spending the summer with his friend Byron Ferguson, whom he called Fergie. They would play tetherball and Ping-Pong and softball and chess. In the evenings they would go to movies or sit on the Dixons' front porch and drink lemonade and listen to spooky shows on the radio. Now the professor was giving him a chance to do something different, and his curiosity was aroused. But Johnny had a timid side—a very large one—and a hundred questions and doubts came crowding into his mind.

"Professor," he asked, in a hesitant voice, "did—didn't you say that you couldn't take anyone with you to help keep up the estate this summer?"

The professor smiled slyly. "I can't take any *paid* help—the will is quite specific about that. But I'm not going to pay you boys. No, indeed! You're going to do things for free, if you feel like doing anything at all. And if the grass grows head high on Perry's estate this summer, I will not care one teensy little bit. Do you think we can rope Byron into this trip?"

Johnny nodded enthusiastically. He and his friend Fergie were practically inseparable, and he would have been unhappy to go on a trip without him. He was sure that he could persuade him to come along.

As the last days of May sped past, plans for the trip were put in order. Johnny's grandparents and Mr. and Mrs. Ferguson liked the professor and trusted him, and they were pleased to have the boys traveling under his care. The boys were excited about the trip, and since they had heard that there was a lot of wilderness around Perry's estate, they got together their camping equipment and aired out their sleeping bags. At the Merrimack Sporting Goods Shop the professor bought a Coleman lamp, an outdoor cookstove, and an enormous pyramid-shaped tent with mosquito-net windows and a front porch that could be propped up on poles. The boys got giggly whenever they thought about camping out with the professor, because they were sure he would be the world's worst outdoorsman. But when he lectured them about whittling tent stakes and making a fire with flint and steel, they always remained very sober faced and grave. Secretly Fergie and Johnny planned to bring along plenty of matches and some nice smooth factory-made tent stakes from Sears and Roebuck.

At the end of the second week of June the professor and his two friends were ready to go. They climbed into the old battered maroon Pontiac and headed north. They sped along U.S. Route One, through New Hampshire and on up into Maine. They passed through Portland and then turned onto a gravel road that wound up into the back-country wilderness of northern Maine. For a long time the scenery was not all that terrific—just a lot of medium-sized pine trees growing in sandy soil. But then they saw the humped shapes of the Rangeley Mountains, and the sunlight glittering on the waters of Lake Mooslookmeguntic.

"Ah, wilderness!" said the professor, waving his hand grandly. "Isn't this beautiful?"

The boys nodded and tried to make appreciative noises. Actually they were both wondering if Perry Childermass's mansion had lights and running water and a refrigerator. Like most young boys they liked camping out, but they wanted the comforts of home when they got sick of roughing it.

The gravel road took them into Stone Arabia, a small town with one movie theater, two gas stations, a church and a general store, and not much else. The professor stopped at a Gulf station to get gas and directions to Perry's estate. Then he drove over a bumpy tarred road and around endless twists and turns. At one bend they almost got run off the road by a teenager in a pickup truck who was careening along at a high speed and playing his radio at an earsplitting volume.

"Young idiot!" growled the professor as he went peeling around the next curve. "They ought to take away his license and the distributor cap on his engine!"

Johnny and Fergie looked at each other and smirked. They knew what a terror the professor could be when he got behind the wheel, and they had always thought it was funny that he didn't have the faintest idea of what a lousy driver he was.

"Uh . . . Prof," asked Fergie, after a while, "how far is it to this place of your brother's? I need a bathroom, and then I think we all oughta go to some burger joint and eat."

The professor pursed up his lips. "You should learn patience, Byron—it is a very great virtue. But to answer your question, it shouldn't be too far. We just passed an old barn with a Mail Pouch chewing tobacco ad on it, and I remember that it was there when I visited Perry about fourteen years ago. The barn was not far from the entrance to—aha! See, there it is, up ahead!"

Fergie and Johnny looked and, sure enough, at the top of the next hill they saw two cement gateposts. As they got closer, they saw that the gateposts were covered with seashells, which must have been stuck into the cement when it was still wet. Two rusty iron gates closed off the driveway that led to the mansion, and they were fastened by a chain and a padlock. Bolted to one gatepost was a greenish bronze plate that said CHILDERMASS.

The professor pulled up in front of the gates and shut off the car's engine. After a little fumbling in his jacket pocket he came up with a small key that he used to undo the padlock. The gates squealed loudly as he shoved them apart, and a few startled birds rose out of the overgrown shrubbery that grew nearby. With an odd little half-smile on his face the professor walked back to the car, got in, and started the engine. They drove up the bumpy, twisting driveway. Behind the wall of bushes, they could see statues and obelisks.

"My brother liked decorations," said the professor with a quiet chuckle. "Every few years he would take a trip to Europe and return with the worst collection of junk that you could imagine. A Greek-god statue or a Roman emperor—he would buy it and have it shipped back to his estate. The stuff is not only ugly, it's absolutely worthless!"

The car jolted on. At last the boys and the professor saw the mansion, a big rectangular stone building with a fancy balustrade along the top. A tall tower capped by a greenish copper roof stood at one corner. In the distance a wildly overgrown flower garden could be seen, and to the left of the house stood a dignified stone tomb. The air was still, and the whole place looked very lonely and deserted.

"So here we are!" said the professor, as he climbed out of the car. With a little sad shake of his head he looked around and then walked quickly toward the tomb. The boys followed him.

The massive bronze doors of the tomb were flanked by two Grecian columns, and the Childermass name was chiseled on the cornice. A few feet from the entrance stood a white marble statue of a bearded man in old-fashioned formal dress. He held a top hat and gloves in one hand, and with his other hand he pointed at the tomb. On the base of the statue was carved one Latin word: RESURGAM.

The professor stopped in front of the statue. He looked it up and down and sighed, and then he fished a cigarette out of the box in his jacket pocket and lit it. "In case you were wondering, boys," he said, as he smoked, "this is Perry—or rather, a pretty good likeness of him. And the Latin word means *I shall rise again*. Perry planned the statue and the tomb, because he had the odd idea that they would help him communicate with the living after he was gone. He really believed that the dead can revisit the earth and talk to the living." He laughed uncomfortably and then added, "I suppose we'll find out if Perry's theories are correct if we stay around here very long."

Johnny glanced quickly off into the shrubbery. He didn't know what kind of person Perry Childermass had been, but he did not want to meet his ghost. Fergie smirked when he saw Johnny's nervousness. He was a no-nonsense type who always thought that weird events could be explained scientifically. Johnny noticed Fergie's grin and he immediately got upset.

"Aw, come on, Fergie!" he said irritably. "If you saw a ghost you'd have the same kind of reaction I would!"

Fergie gazed steadily at his friend. "Maybe I would, John baby, and maybe I wouldn't. But I'll tell you one thing—"

"Oh, gentlemen, please stop!" exclaimed the professor, cutting him off. "It is much too hot a day for a senseless argument about spooks and specters. Why don't the two of you help me drag our luggage indoors, and then we'll go hunt up that burger joint that Fergie saw on the way here. Ghosts are one thing, but tummy-rumbles are quite another, and I am starved!"

The boys grinned and followed the professor out to the car. It took three trips, but finally they had the bed-rolls and the tent and the Coleman lamp and everything else piled up in the front hallway of the old mansion. The hall smelled musty, and all the pictures and furniture were covered with a thick furry layer of dust. Johnny and Fergie peered into one or two of the rooms that opened off the hall, but they had that shut-up smell too, and the furniture in them was covered with sheets. As the professor had said on the way up, it would take a bit of work to make this old dump livable again. Oh, well—that could all be done tomorrow. Eagerly the boys followed the professor out to the car, and they drove back to Stone Arabia and gorged on chili burgers and fries at Big Ed's Steak House. As they drove home the weather began to change. The air got chilly, and dark clouds rushed in to cover the sky. When the three travelers got back to the old mansion, the place looked more grim and forlorn than ever, and gloom descended on them. Frantically the professor searched his mind for something that would be fun to do, and then he remembered a part of the estate that he hadn't thought about in years.

"Come on, boys!" he said, as he sprang out of the car. "I want to show you something!"

Fergie and Johnny followed the professor down some stone steps and through the weedy garden to a place where the ground dropped away suddenly. A brick retaining wall marked the end of the garden, and beyond it lay a long sloping lawn that looked like the fairway on a golf course. At the far end of the lawn a tall red granite column rose into the sky. It seemed to be topped by a statue, but at this distance it was hard to tell.

Fergie and Johnny rushed to the wall to stare. "Get a load of *that*!" exclaimed Fergie in amazement. "What is it?"

"Oh, that is just one of the lovely ornaments that my wacky brother added to his wonderful estate," said the professor with a careless shrug. "It is a column in honor of General Nicholas Herkimer, who won the Battle of Oriskany in the year 1777. He and a bunch of ragtag militiamen beat the British redcoats led by Colonel Barry St. Leger. The battle took place in the Mohawk Valley, which is many hundreds of miles from here, and please don't ask me why my dear brother was so interested in General Herkimer—he just was, that's all. The column is three hundred feet high, and you actually can walk up the inside of it. Come on—let's go have a closer look."

The boys followed the professor along the brick wall to a place where a long concrete staircase descended to the grassy plain below. They walked down the steps and then started the long trek toward the column. The afternoon sun had broken through the gray clouds that were piling up in the sky, and long shafts of reddish light fell across the grass. On they plodded, till finally they stood at the base of the column. A bolt-studded iron door was set into the stonework, and it appeared to be locked. But the professor had a key, and after he had shoved the groaning door inward, the three of them began to climb the endless spiralling stair. The flinty steps would up and up, and the air inside the column was stifling and hot. Finally, after an exhausting trek, the climbers saw light shining through a narrow slit in the stone. After a few more steps they were out on the round platform at the top of the column. Above them towered the pigeon-streaked statue of General Herkimer, who brandished his sword bravely and waved his imaginary troops onward. They looked out at the vast rolling landscape. Behind them lay the mansion, and to the right was a small part of Lake Umbagog. The late sunlight stained the water orange, and a small domed building stood on a wooded cliff overlooking the lake.

"Hey, what's that?" Fergie asked, as he pointed. "Is it a temple or something?"

The professor smiled and shook his head. "No, Byron, that is another of the odd little surprises that this estate contains. It is an observatory. My charming brother got interested in astronomy about twenty years ago, so he built that domed thingamajig and equipped it with a large telescope. He used to go up there to study the stars and look for comets, but one night—believe it or not—a falling meteorite hit the telescope's lens and shattered it. Well, my brother took that as a sign from heaven that he ought to stop messing around with astronomy. So he closed up the observatory and padlocked it, and as far as I know no one's been in there in the last ten years."

Johnny looked puzzled. "Professor," he said hesitantly, "that part about the meteorite being a sign from heaven—it might be true, you know. I mean, what are the chances of something like that happening, just by accident?"

"Pretty darned small," said the professor, as he drummed his fingers on the balcony's rusty rail. "However, I wouldn't jump to conclusions if I were you. That 'meteorite' may have been someone with a twenty-two rifle. *Anyway*, I'll take you and Fergie over there sometime. The place has probably gone to ruin, but it might be worth exploring." He paused and yawned hugely. "As for myself," he said sleepily, "I feel like going back to the old manse for a little rest. It's been a long, hard day of driving, and these old bones ain't what they used to be. Perry had a TV set installed a few years ago, and there are some nice comfortable chairs in the study. Why don't we go back and collapse?"

Fergie and Johnny nodded wearily, and the three of them began the long march back down the column. As they walked toward the mansion, a cold wind began to blow. Once again the sky clouded over, and a fine drizzling mist fell. By the time they got back to the mansion, they were exhausted. The rooms of the old house seemed cold and clammy, and when the professor tried to turn the heat on, nothing happened. So they all gathered in the book-lined study, and the professor built a fire in the fireplace. The TV was working fine, and the boys got some Cokes out of the refrigerator and returned to the study, where they dumped themselves into two big sagging armchairs. The professor perched on the couch, put his feet up on the coffee table, and lit a Balkan Sobranie cigarette. Heavy rain began to beat against the dusty windows, but in the firelit room everything seemed cozy and homelike. The television show was a rerun of *The Web*, a spooky mystery show that the professor liked.

"There now, boys," he said lazily, as he blew a thin stream of smoke out of his mouth, "you see that roughing it in the northern wilderness is not so bad after all. Tomorrow we will go shopping and lay in some supplies, and then—*good God, what was that?*"

The boys jumped and then looked quickly at the professor. "What is it?" asked Johnny excitedly. "What happened?"

The professor didn't know what to say. He had glanced off to his right, toward one of the rain-streaked windows, and he had seen a face pressed to the glass. The face had been blurred and shadowy, but it definitely had been there. And then, a second later, it was gone.

The professor was on his feet in a second, and he dashed to the window. Bravely he threw up the sash and peered out, but all he saw was darkness, wind, and rain. *"Blast!"* he roared, as he slammed the sash down. "There was somebody out there! Someone snooping about the estate. I'm going to go out there and give him a piece of my mind!"

The boys were alarmed. If there was a man out there, he might have a gun. What would the professor do?

The professor glanced quickly at the boys, and he read their thoughts. "Oh, don't be such scaredy-cats!" he said. "It's not Machine Gun Kelly, it's just some local dimwit who thinks it's fun to peer in people's windows. I'll be back in a jiffy."

And with that the professor snatched his flashlight up off the library table and ran out into the hall. The boys followed him, and soon all three were tramping across the loudly squealing boards of the front porch. They clattered down the porch steps and ran across the slippery wet flagstone walk to the muddy driveway where the old Pontiac sat. Wildly the professor waved his flashlight around, and he shouted some rather unpleasant names into the darkness. But if there had been any-one there, he was gone now.

"Miserable clot!" growled the professor. "I would have enjoyed giving him a good talking-to. Oh, well! It's good riddance I sup—"

The professor's voice died. He had been waving his flashlight around as he talked, and the long pale beam had swept across the front of Perry's tomb. What he saw made him stop and stare: the two wrought-iron gates on the front of the tomb were hanging open.

For about half a minute the professor just stood and looked. Then, with the boys close behind him, he marched forward till he stood before the gloomy little stone house. On the walk at the foot of the stairs lay the chain that had fastened the gates. Picking it up with a muttered curse, the professor trotted up the steps of the tomb and examined the bronze inner doors.

"Merciful heavens! This is worse than I thought!" he muttered. "The doors are ajar! Now, who on earth . . ."

The professor shoved one door open and quickly played the beam of his light around. The coffin was in its place, and everything seemed the way it should be. With a sudden angry jerk the professor pulled the doors shut and twisted the handle that latched them. He closed the iron gates and loosely fastened them with the iron chain, and then he began to stalk grimly back to the house. The boys could not see the expression on his face, but they knew he was shaken and upset.

CHAPTER THREE

That night the professor and the boys slept on the floor of the study. While the rain rattled on the window-panes, they lay snug in their sleeping bags and tried to forget about the scary thing that had happened earlier that evening. The professor did not get much sleep—he lay awake most of the night listening to the rain and hoping that he would not see any more ghostly faces. Around five in the morning he gave up trying to sleep and went out to the wide front porch, where he sat smoking cigarettes till dawn. When they woke up, Fergie and Johnny washed up in the kitchen sink and helped the professor make breakfast on the old black iron gas range. The boys were in a cheerful mood, and they were itching to explore the crumbling, run-down estate. The professor stayed moody for most of the morning, because he was convinced that he had seen his dead brother's ghost. Later, though, he began to cheer up. A repair-man arrived and went to the basement to fix the broken oil burner, and this was definitely a step in the right direction. As he sat in the sunlit kitchen, sipping coffee and listening to the pinging and banging that came from below, the professor began to feel that everything might just possibly work out all right.

After lunch Fergie and Johnny went out to play flies and grounders on the long sloping back lawn. The professor went upstairs and began to explore the many rooms of the vast echoing old mansion. As he plodded along the gloomy corridors, he tried to imagine his brother living all alone in this place. "He must have been out of his ever-loving mind," said the professor to himself as he kicked at the worn hall carpet. He walked up a narrow staircase to the tower room on the third floor. At the top of the stairs was a tall, pointed doorway. The heavy black oak door hung ajar, but beyond lay darkness. How very odd, thought the professor as he stepped into the room. He fumbled for the light switch, and the bare bulb in the ceiling fixture came on. Now the professor understood why the room was so dark. The windows were boarded up. Quickly he looked around the small circular room—it was bare and desolate, and smelled strongly of dust. A brick fireplace was built into one wall, and above the mantel a metal disk was bolted to the wall. This was a stovepipe-hole cover. Apparently at one time there had been a woodstove in the room, and the smoke had gotten out through a pipe that ran into the fireplace's chimney. On the disk a pleasant scene of fields and trees had been painted, and it made the professor smile, because he liked old-fashioned things.

Humming quietly, he began to poke around the room. Not really much to see, was there? Off in a far corner, beyond the fireplace, was a closet door. He opened it, half hoping that a body would fall out. But all he saw were some old warped golf clubs and a slab of varnished wood. Reaching in, he pulled the piece of wood out and turned it over. To his surprise he saw chessboard squares! But the board was very warped, and unusable. "What on earth . . ." said the professor quietly, and he walked out into the middle of the room holding the bizarre object that he had found. Some very peculiar thoughts began to run through his mind. He remembered the first two lines of the weird poem that had been included in his dead brother's letter:

Why a dead eye in a room with no view?
Why pallid dwarves on a board that's not true?

This shuttered room definitely had no view, and in his hands he was holding a chessboard that was warped—not true, in other words. But what was the dead eye? He didn't see any around, and he hoped that he never would. As for the "pallid dwarves," they ought to be chessmen, and it certainly was true that ivory chessmen were pale or pallid, but—but what? Pacing nervously back and forth, the professor tried to think, but the more he thought the more confused he got. "It's all in my mind," he grumbled, as he carried the board back to the closet and propped it up in a corner. "I've just made up something to entertain myself with, and if I'm not careful I'll drive myself batty!" Sighing, he closed the closet door and wiped his dusty hands on his trousers. He left the room and trotted down the stairs, but at the first landing he paused and peered anxiously over his shoulder at the dark doorway above him. "I wonder . . . he muttered thoughtfully. "I really wonder!"

The professor spent the rest of the afternoon doing mindless tasks—he oiled the old hand-powered lawn mower in the garage and actually managed to shove it back and forth on the grass a few times. Then he went down to the cellar of the mansion to see how the repairman was doing, and he got there just in time to hear the oil burner roar into life. This was great, because it meant that he and his friends would not have to huddle in sleeping bags tonight—they would be able to sleep in real beds on soft mattresses, with clean sheets and pillowcases. After he had paid the repairman, the professor went out to the back lawn and sat down to watch the boys as they batted balls in the air and caught them. He sighed with contentment. Tonight they would drive back to the town of Stone Arabia and eat at Big Ed's and go to a movie. When they got back to their nice comfy warm house, life would seem better than it had for some time.

Big Ed's burgers were as good as they had been be-fore, and the Cornel Wilde pirate movie at the Mecca Theater was exciting, so by the time Fergie, Johnny, and the professor piled into the car and headed for home, they felt tired and happy. The car sped along dark, winding roads and finally turned into the driveway where the two tall stone gateposts loomed. As they bumped and jounced toward the mansion, the professor found that he was getting more and more nervous. He felt a sense of foreboding, as if something awful was going to happen. Normally he would have shrugged the feeling off, but some pretty uncanny things had happened since the three of them arrived at Perry's estate, and it was possible that more unpleasant surprises were on the way. Fireflies winked among the bushes, and brief flashes of heat lightning glowed above the clouds that hung over the old mansion. On they drove.

"We're not gonna need that furnace tonight, Prof," Fergie said. "I'm sweatin' bullets, an' I guess you guys are too. You shouldn't of paid that guy to fix it. We could get through the summer without a furnace, I'll bet."

"Oh, really?" growled the professor. "If you're such an expert on Maine weather, Byron, I would suggest that you rent yourself out to a local radio station. But I will bet you five dollars that we will have some pretty chilly nights before this summer is over. Remember, we have to stay here until . . ."

The professor's voice died, and he jammed on the

brakes. The long pale beams of the car's headlights had picked out something in the distance. Something that was wrong. At a bend in the drive a flagstone path began. It led to the door of the gloomy stone house where Peregrine Childermass lay buried. On the winding track of pale stones a shapeless dark lump lay. Silently the professor shut off the car's motor and got out. He trotted up the path, turned on his flashlight, and stooped over the object. It was a black tailcoat, the kind that people sometimes wear to weddings. With a shock the professor recognized the coat—it was the one that Perry had owned. Stooping, the professor grasped a lapel and saw the Masonic pin. Then he reached inside and found the label: *Pine Tree State Tailors. Bangor, Maine.* It was definitely Perry's coat—no doubt about that. Probably it was the one he had been buried in.

With a strange look on his face the professor walked up the path, playing the beam of his flashlight before him. Fergie and Johnny followed a few steps behind. They were curious, but they were not quite as fearless as the professor was. At last the three of them stopped outside the entrance to the ornate stone tomb. There stood Perry's statue, smiling weirdly at them and pointing toward the door. But the wrought-iron gates had once again been wrenched open, and on the broad marble steps lay an open coffin. The lid lay nearby, and it was cracked and splintered, as if someone had forced it loose with a crowbar.

"Heavenly days, McGee!" the professor whispered in

an awestruck tone. "It looks as if a ghoul has been wandering around. I cannot imagine . . ." His voice trailed off as he bent over the empty coffin and touched the quilted lining with his fingers. Then, with a haunted look in his eyes, he turned back to the boys. "I'm afraid that mischief is afoot," he announced solemnly. "Mischief and dirty dealing and the Lord knows what! Who on earth would be so rotten as to steal my poor brother's corpse? *Who?*"

Fergie threw a quick look at Johnny and shrugged. "You got me, Prof!" he said, folding his arms solemnly. "I used to read about body snatchers, but they were people who stole corpses so medical students could work on them. But that was in the old days."

The professor nodded. "You're right," he said grimly. "So why was my brother's tomb violated? I really would like to know!"

For quite some time the professor and the two boys stood there in the dark. While the crickets chirped loudly in the tall grass behind the mausoleum, they talked in whispers about grave robbers and the face at the window and whether or not the police ought to be notified. On one thing they were in complete agreement—something very strange was going on.

With a gloomy sigh the professor glanced at the gaping door of the looted tomb.

"Better go turn the car lights off," muttered the professor. "Ghouls or no ghouls, it's time for some shut-eye. We can call the cops in the morning."

Johnny and Fergie followed the professor back to the car. When he had shut off the headlights he led the way to the front door of the house. The lamp that burned behind the fanlight seemed very friendly to the boys, who kept glancing nervously over their shoulders to see if anyone was following them. Once they were inside, they helped the professor with the two heavy sliding bolts that secured the top and bottom of the stout oak door, and then they went upstairs to bed. The professor was still feeling pretty upset, so he went to the kitchen and played solitaire until he began to feel calmer. The ticking of the old Waterbury shelf clock and the hum of the refrigerator relaxed him. He poured himself a shot of brandy from the silver-plated pint flask he had brought with him. After downing the fiery liquid in one gulp he shut off the lights and walked up the broad staircase, humming tunelessly. But instead of going to his bedroom he went to the narrow flight of steps that led to the tower room. The professor really didn't know why he wanted to go to that eerie boarded-up chamber. He just felt a powerful urge, as if someone were shoving him from behind, making him go. With the beam of his flashlight showing the way, he stomped up the dusty steps till he stood once again before the gloomy paneled door. There was a hall light here, but when he flipped the switch, the professor got a little bluish flash and then darkness—the bulb had burned out. With a muttered curse the professor opened the door of the room, reached inside, and pushed a small black button. The overhead bulb came on, and he went on in.

In the middle of the floor the professor paused. *Why did this place upset him so much?* He found that he was breathing heavily, and his heart was hammering. The room was ugly and depressing—no doubt about that. But there really wasn't anything evil or frightening here that he could see. He had felt bad enough the first time he came here, but now he felt worse—much worse. The grim boarded windows seemed like dark portals that might suddenly fly open and let in . . . let in what? The professor had no idea. He tried to hum, but the humming died in his throat. He walked over to the painted metal disk that was bolted to the fireplace chimney. He stared at it fixedly, and the longer he stared, the stranger he felt. It was as if waves of power were coming from the disk, waves as strong as the heat from a heat lamp. He had the peculiar feeling that the cheerful little scene of trees and flowery fields was just a mask that hid something horrible from view. And—strangest of all— he had the very powerful impression that someone was staring at him from behind the painted disk. It was a very unsettling feeling, and he kept trying to fight it down, but the feeling kept coming back. This is very foolish, the professor told himself. But still he had to struggle against the urge to go and kneel down on the hearth and peer up the fireplace's chimney. What did he expect to see? Nothing, probably. This is a lot of dratted poppycock! thought the professor, and with a shuddering sigh he pulled himself together and marched out of the room, slamming the door behind him.

CHAPTER FOUR

The next morning the professor called up the police in Stone Arabia and told them about the break-in. Around ten, two policemen showed up in a rusty squad car, took notes, asked questions, and peered into the empty tomb. The professor was glad when the two men finally left. He was convinced that the police would not find a clue. In the mysteries he read the cops never solved anything. He was sure that things would work out the same in real life.

Days passed. The professor brought in supplies and stocked the refrigerator with food. Meanwhile the boys did more exploring. Several times they hiked out to the Herkimer Column, and one afternoon they even climbed the wooded bluff to have a look at the abandoned observatory. Unfortunately the door of the building was padlocked tight, but the boys peered up at the greenish copper dome that covered the broken telescope. The concrete walls of the circular building were covered with kids' initials and smart-alecky remarks. The whole place looked as if it had been neglected for years, and the boys wondered why Perry Childermass had wanted to build it in the first place. They didn't hang around the observatory long, however—the professor was frying porterhouse steaks for dinner that night, and the boys started feeling hungry.

One night late in June something odd happened.

Johnny, Fergie, and the professor had gone to see a movie in Stone Arabia. The theater was air conditioned, and sitting in it was a delightful relief from the hot muggy air outside. Finally, when they had to leave, they grumbled a bit about the weather and then headed down the street to their parked car. As they walked, Johnny and Fergie suddenly noticed a very strange-looking man coming toward them. His face was round and ruddy, and he sported a well-trimmed mustache with waxed upturned tips. He wore an ulster, which is a kind of British overcoat with a half cape that comes down to the elbows, and under his arm he carried a small black leather case. The professor did not see the man at all—he was walking along with his head down, as he did sometimes. As they passed, the man in the overcoat stepped sideways to avoid the professor, and at that moment he coughed. At the sound of the cough the professor's head snapped up, and he muttered "Excuse me!" He stepped sideways, thinking that he was getting out of the man's way, but instead he slammed straight into him. The man made an indignant noise and stepped backward, dropping the case he was carrying. The lid popped open, and a dozen small white chessmen spilled onto the sidewalk. The chessmen weren't the ordinary kind that you see in stores. These looked like little men and women, with bug eyes and glum expressions on their faces. They were intricately carved from ivory, or maybe bone, and they looked as if they belonged in a museum.

In a flash the man in the overcoat fell to his knees and began frantically scooping the chessmen back into the leather case. When the professor stepped forward to help him, the man looked up with a wild look of anger and fear.

 "Get away from me, you fool!" he snarled.

Quickly the professor glanced at the boys, and then the three of them ducked around the lamppost and marched on down the street toward their car. Fergie threw a scornful glance over his shoulder.

"Boy, was that guy ever a grouch!" he muttered with a shake of his head. "And what is he doing wearing an overcoat on a night like this?"

The professor grinned. "Some people have thin blood," he said. "I had a cousin who never could get warm, even when it was ninety out. As for your other comment, I'd say you're right—that character makes me look sweet and lovable by comparison. People bump into each other all the time, and it's not a cause for nuclear war. By the way, what did you think of those . . ."

The professor's voice died. A line from Perry's crazy little poem had suddenly popped into his head. *Why pallid dwarves on a board that's not true?* When the professor stopped speaking, the boys turned and looked strangely at him.

"What's the matter, Professor?" asked Johnny, anxiously.

The professor forced himself to smile and shrug carelessly. "Oh, nothing. Really it wasn't anything terribly important. I was just wondering if I left the gas turned on—on the kitchen stove, I mean. But you know me: I'm always fussing about something."

As the professor stooped to unlock the car door, the boys exchanged glances. They were pretty sure that the professor was covering up some secret worry. Did it have to do with the man they had just seen? Whatever the problem was, the boys knew very well that they wouldn't get anything out of the old man by pushing and prodding. When he was good and ready, he would tell them what was on his mind.

They drove back to the estate in silence. In the distance heat lightning flashed, outlining the jagged edges of storm clouds. Finally the car pulled up in front of the old mansion. As he stepped out, the professor looked up, and then he gasped—there was a light on in the tower room! Although the windows were boarded, there were cracks between the boards, and lamplight shone through them.

In a flash the professor turned to the boys, who were standing on the other side of the car. "Has one of you been fooling around in that tower room?" he snapped.

"Not me, Prof!" said Fergie. "Why would I wanta go up there?"

"I haven't been up there at all," said Johnny firmly. He was scared of the place and wouldn't go anywhere near it.

The professor stared a long time at the two boys. "Well, *somebody* has been fooling around up there!" he said irritably. "I distinctly remember shutting that light off. Ah, well! Maybe it's ghosts." He laughed uncomfortably.

The three travelers went inside and ate a late supper at the kitchen table. No one said much, but as he was going upstairs to bed, Johnny turned and said, "Professor?"

"Yes? What is it, John?"

"Are you gonna go up and turn off that light?"

The old man turned pale, and he tried hard to hide his nervousness. "I intend to let the stupid thing burn all night, and then shut it off in the morning," he said primly. "I don't think our electric bill will go through the roof because of one crummy sixty-watt bulb."

Later, up in his bedroom, Johnny was getting ready to turn in for the night. He sat in a high-backed chair and looked around at the heavy oak furniture, the worn

Persian carpet, and the fancy light fixtures with their tulip-shaped blown-glass shades. As he let his eyes wander, he thought about the odd and frightening things that had happened since they came to this place. What did it all mean? Was there a pattern to everything or was it all just coincidence? Johnny sighed discontentedly—this was not a case where thinking helped very much. Barefoot, he padded down the hall to the big old-fashioned bathroom and washed his face in the marble sink. When he was back in his room, he climbed into bed, took off his glasses, and turned off the lamp that stood on the mahogany night table. Down Johnny sank onto the feather pillow, and for a moment he had a blurry vision of long linen curtains moving slowly in the pale moonlight. Then he was asleep.

Johnny wasn't sure who or what it was that awoke him. But he sat up with a start, as if someone had shaken him. Blearily he looked around, and with his right hand he fumbled for the glasses that lay neatly folded on the bedside table. Finally he put them on and looked again: the bureau and chairs were lost in shadow, and a long streak of moonlight lay on the rug. Straining his eyes, Johnny peered into the dark. To his horror he saw that somebody was standing in the shadows at the other end of the room. A breath of air from the open window carried an unpleasant smell toward him—a smell of mold, and earth, and the grave. The figure moved, and it spoke in a hoarse, croaking voice.

"Don't let him do it. Stop him if you can."

Johnny stared. He felt his blood roaring in his ears, and he was afraid he might faint. The figure took a step forward, and Johnny was horribly afraid it was coming to get him. But at that instant the shape melted into smoke and drifted away out of the open window. For a long time Johnny sat rigid with terror, his back pressed against the high carved headboard of the bed. Minutes dragged past, but finally Johnny's heart began to beat normally again. He wiped the sweat off his face with his sleeve and closed his eyes, trying hard to get rid of the ghastly vision that still hovered in his brain. Should he go down to the professor's room and wake him up and tell him what had happened? But what if he met the figure again in the dark corridor? Or what if it was crouching by the side of the professor's bed? Slowly Johnny slid down onto his mattress. He rolled over onto his side and tried to sleep, but sleep was a long time coming. Gradually, though, weariness overcame him, and he drifted off.

The next morning, when he woke up, Johnny wondered if he had just had a bad dream. He knew that you couldn't always tell the difference between sleeping and waking, but still . . . well, maybe he'd better let the professor decide.

When he got down to the kitchen, Johnny found that the professor was trying to make toast in Perry's antique toaster. Even though he was rich, Perry Childermass had kept a lot of 1930's-style equipment in his house, and the toaster was one of those things with openwork wire sides, the kind where you have to do the toast one side at a time and then turn it over. Gingerly, with a pot holder in one hand, the professor took the toast out and turned it—and then he dropped it on the floor.

"Drat!" he growled. "Why did my idiotic brother fill his house with things that ought to be in a museum or—oh, hello, John. How are you? You don't look as if you slept very well last night."

Johnny smiled wanly. Then, with a lot of hemming and hawing, he sat down and told the professor about the frightening experience he had had last night. The professor listened with a solemn look on his face, and he nodded occasionally or shook his head. When Johnny had finished speaking, the professor was silent for a while. Then he picked up a knife and began to butter his toast.

"I'd like to think you had a bad dream," he said slowly, "but in view of the events that have happened since we got here I'd say that was just wishful thinking. I went up to the tower room this morning and turned that blasted light off, and I looked around, but I couldn't find anything wrong. Nevertheless, something very strange and sinister is going on, and I wish I could figure out what it is. Maybe it is connected with that weird poem that my brother sent me. I honestly don't know what to think! But I wish to *heaven* that some ghostly messenger would arrive and tell us, plainly, without a lot of double-talk, what is going to happen! I *hate* riddles!"

Johnny went to the refrigerator and poured himself a

glass of milk. "Do you think I really saw a ghost?" he asked, as he turned around.

The professor shrugged. "You may have. You may even have seen the spirit of my dear departed brother. And what was it he said? 'Stop him,' or some such thing? Stop who from doing what? Do you see what I mean? We know something, but we just don't know *enough*!"

At this point Fergie came running in from the front hall. He was pale and he looked very upset. "Hey, you guys! I found something outside. It's really kind of awful! Come and look at it!"

CHAPTER FIVE

Johnny and the professor were startled. They followed Fergie out to the wildly overgrown garden behind the house. At one time the place had probably been well kept and very pretty, but it had gone to ruin. The rose bushes were wildly overgrown, and so were the privet hedges. Tall weeds had choked the tulips and zinnias, which lay dead across the stone paths, and bindweed climbed the trellises where the hollyhocks were supposed to be. At the far end of the garden four marble pillars rose. On top of each one was the plaster bust of a Roman emperor: Otho, Vitellius, Trajan, and Hadrian were the names chiseled on the bases of the four busts. But the bust of Hadrian was gone. It lay in shattered fragments at the base of the column it had stood on. This was the thing that Fergie had brought them to see, and as they hurried along the weedy paths, he tried to give an explanation.

". . . and so I was battin' a ball in the air, an' I hit this line drive, an' it hit that statue, an' . . . well, Prof, I'm sorry about what happened, but—"

"Please spare me your apologies, Byron," snapped the professor. "Those busts are next door to worthless, and I wouldn't mind if you spent the day heaving rocks at them. But is that what you've brought us out here to see? Pieces of broken plaster?"

"No, Prof, there's something worse than that. Come on an' have a look!"

Without any more talk Johnny and the professor followed Fergie to the base of the column where the bust had once stood. Among the weeds lay pieces of broken plaster, and in the middle of everything, staring grimly up at them, was a human skull.

Johnny gasped, and the professor sucked in his breath with a hiss. "My God!" he exclaimed, as he bent to inspect the skull. "Do you mean to say that this was *inside* the bust?"

Fergie nodded. "Yeah, it was. If you look close, you'll see that there's little bits of plaster stickin' to the skull. Why would anyone do a thing like that?"

The professor grimaced. "Interesting question," he muttered, as he turned the skull over in his hands. "This place gets weirder by the minute, doesn't it? Hmm . . . I wonder who this belonged to. Maybe I should give the police a call. But do we really want those oafs trampling about here again? Probably not." He looked up suddenly. "Gentlemen, can you amuse yourselves for the rest of the morning while I go down to the public library in Stone Arabia? I'll see you later."

Before Johnny or Fergie could say anything, the professor tucked the skull under his arm and marched off toward the house.

"Hey!" exclaimed Fergie, as he watched the old man go. "He's got a bug in his ear about something, that's for sure! What do you think he's gonna do at the library?"

Johnny bit his lip. "I don't know, but you can be sure we'll find out about it if he does turn up something."

For the rest of the morning Johnny and Fergie played flies and grounders. Finally, around noon, they went up to the house for a glass of lemonade, and they were sipping and talking on the front porch when the professor's car came rattling up the drive. Out he sprang, and slam went the car door. As he walked toward the house, the boys saw that he had a funny little half smile on his face. Had he found out anything? It was hard to tell.

The professor walked into the house without a word. A few minutes later he came out with a large glass of ice water in his hand. Sighing, he sat down on a rocking chair and wiped his forehead with his sleeve.

"Hot, isn't it?" he said, after he had taken a few sips. "I hear it may turn into a heat wave, if this weather goes on long enough."

Fergie gave the professor an irritated glance. "Cut the comedy, Prof. Tell us if you found out anything. Come on!"

The professor shrugged. "Well, I did and I didn't. I wanted to find out if there was any record of graves being desecrated recently. So I dug into the files of the local newspaper for the last five years, but I found out absolutely nothing! It's odd, you know—I mean, that skull had to come from *somewhere*!"

"Maybe the skull got stolen a long time ago," Johnny suggested. "That's possible, isn't it?"

The professor thought a bit. "Well, it *could* have been stolen many years ago, but it wasn't put into that plaster head until recently. You see, anything made of plaster gets all dirty and pitted when it has been left out in the weather for a while. Those busts are all pretty clean."

"Do you think there are skulls inside all of those heads?" asked Fergie excitedly. The idea seemed to fascinate him, and he grinned wickedly.

The professor pursed up his lips. "I have no idea," he said sourly, "and I am not going to bash those other three heads open in order to find out. The point is, we don't know who belongs to that skull that you found. However, I did find out something when I was rooting around in the library. The British Museum in London was robbed about two weeks ago. And do you know what got stolen? Some of the little carved chessmen from the Isle of Lewis. They're eight hundred years old, and they're made from walrus tusks, and they were found

) 46 (

in a sandbank on that lonely little island off the north-west coast of Scotland. And do you know what? They look just like—"

"The chessmen that creep was carryin' in his leather case!" exclaimed Fergie, cutting in eagerly.

The professor gave Fergie a wry glance. "You're way ahead of me, Sherlock," he said. "Yes, the chessmen that fell out on the sidewalk looked like the ones from the British Museum. I don't believe it's a coincidence either—that man in the overcoat has to be the thief that the British authorities are after. But what I want to know is this: *Why* is he up here? What is he doing? And does it have anything to do with that stupid poem my brother sent me?"

Fergie took a long drink of lemonade and stared out across the lawn, which was shimmering in the noontime heat. "Would you recite that poem again, Prof? I don't remember it all, but I'll bet you've got it memorized by now."

"Indeed I do," said the professor crisply.

> "Why a dead eye in a room with no view?
> Why pallid dwarves on a board that's not true?
> To pull the hairy stars from their nest
> And give sinful humans a well-deserved test.

"A lot of the pieces of this puzzle are almost fitting together, but there's still a lot that is mysterious: the eyehole of a skull could be a dead eye, couldn't it? The pallid dwarves have to be the chessmen we saw on the sidewalk, and we've found the warped chessboard. So far so good! But what on earth are hairy stars, and what does it mean to 'pull them from their nest'? Are the stars flowers with hairy petals? Are they famous musicians with long hair? Or are they something else? And what is this test that is going to be given to sinful humans? There is a lot here that is just as clear as mud!"

"You forgot about the room with no view," Fergie put in smugly. "It has to be that boarded-up room in the tower. Well, doesn't it?"

The professor glared at Fergie over the tops of his glasses. "Oh, bully for you!" he growled. "Of *course* it's that tower room! I didn't think I had to spell that out! But what is going to happen in that room? And why do I feel so uncomfortable whenever I go up there? That is what I would like to know!"

The professor and the boys talked on about the poem and the skull, but they soon found that they were just talking in circles, so they gave it up. After lunch they went for a hike partway around Lake Umbagog. The professor wore his old khaki walking shorts and his wide-brimmed campaign hat, which made him look like a cranky scoutmaster. He hiked so fast that the boys had trouble keeping up with him, and he babbled endlessly about the plants and trees that grew near the path. Later, when they got home, the three of them played a little tennis on an old crumbling court near the house. Johnny and Fergie took turns against the professor, who was amazingly nimble for a man his age—in fact, he won about half the games they played. Then in the evening they had an outdoor barbecue, and sat around on the porch swapping stories and sipping iced tea until sundown. Though they tried to be cheerful, they kept thinking of the sinister events that had happened at the old estate. A dark cloud hung over their pleasant chatter, and it would not go away.

Late that night Johnny had a very disturbing dream. He dreamed that he got out of bed and floated, weightless, down the broad staircase and out the front door of the mansion. He drifted, his feet barely brushing the wet grass, across the weedy garden and down to the long lawn that led to the Herkimer Column. He swept past the column through clumps of bushes and briars. Branches and two-pronged thistles tore at his pajamas and raked across his face. Finally he was dumped down with a jarring thump, and to his horror he found that he was awake and really, truly standing in the middle of a patch of tall wet grass. Gray moonlight bathed the scene, and when Johnny's foggy brain cleared, he saw that he was near the old abandoned observatory. Crickets chirped loudly, and the moonlight cast a dull sheen on the greenish copper dome that hid a broken telescope. What was he doing here? Why had he been dragged out to this lonely place in the middle of the night? Johnny shivered and clutched his sides, and then he heard it: a crunching in the bushes that grew close to the walls of the half-ruined building.

"Who—who is it?" Johnny whispered hoarsely. His

voice was so strange that it hardly sounded like his own.

No answer. But the crunching went on, and the bushes swayed. Johnny waited, tense and frightened. He was rooted to the spot—he couldn't move. A hunched shape stepped out into the open space in front of the locked door of the observatory. Someone spoke, and in numb horror Johnny listened.

"Crazy Annie has the key," the voice chanted in a high, reedy singsong. *"Stop him before it's too late, stop him before it's too late."*

But Johnny did not hear any more. The moonlit bushes spun around him, and he collapsed, unconscious, on the cold, damp ground.

CHAPTER SIX

When Johnny woke up, it was daylight. Birds twittered in the bushes, and the sun had just barely risen above the misty gray waters of Lake Umbagog. Shaken, wet, and scared, Johnny pulled himself to his feet. His body ached, and his mind was still in a fog. Sluggishly he trudged on down the path and made his way up the long lawn toward the mansion. When he got to the front porch, he smelled bacon and eggs frying, and he knew that the professor must be up. The old man was an early riser, and he was pottering about in the kitchen humming tunelessly to himself. When he saw Johnny, the professor's mouth dropped open. He had assumed that Johnny was still asleep upstairs, but here he was in pajamas that were wet to the knees and covered with thistles. And the glazed, groggy look on Johnny's face was not very reassuring. Where had he been? And why did he look so scared?

"John!" said the professor, turning halfway round with a spatula in his hand. "Do you always go out for early-morning hikes in your p.j.'s? Your grandmother would have a fit if she knew—"

The professor stopped speaking, because Johnny had burst into tears. Immediately the old man dropped his spatula into the cooking eggs and rushed forward. He clutched Johnny and held him while the boy's body was racked with loud, shuddering sobs. In the middle of his crying Johnny kept thinking, I hope Fergie doesn't come down and see me like this! But he really couldn't control himself, and he went on sobbing for quite a long time.

At last Johnny was all cried out, and he slumped into a chair and sat watching listlessly as the professor got him a large glass of water. Johnny grabbed it with both hands and drank greedily. Then, slowly, with lots of starts and stops, he told about his dream and the things he had seen out by the observatory when he was wide awake. The professor listened with a concerned expression on his face, and when Johnny had finished talking, he went to the sink and stared out the little curtained window. Johnny knew that the professor was trying to hide his feelings. He always stared out windows when he didn't want anyone to see the expression on his face.

"Another piece of the puzzle," muttered the professor

in a faraway, dreamy voice. "What on earth does it mean? *Crazy Annie has the key*—that's very clear, isn't it? Clear as mud! What key? What Crazy Annie? If it really is my brother's ghost that is speaking to you, I would like to give him a piece of my mind. He has no business scaring you half to death and dragging you out in the middle of the night so he can babble idiotic riddles into your ear! I wish I knew what was going on!"

"So do I," said Johnny. "Maybe it'll all be clear to us someday."

"Oh, sure!" growled the professor sarcastically. "It'll be clear when it's too late for us to do anything!" Picking up his spatula, the professor began stirring the eggs again. "What I'm trying to say is this," he went on in a low, worried voice. "I think something bad is going to happen around here, but I don't know what it is. We might be able to prevent the evil thing from occurring if we knew more, but we just have a few bits and pieces of a very incomplete jigsaw puzzle. A ghost—my poor brother's ghost, probably—has appeared to you twice, but aside from scaring the socks off you, he doesn't seem to have done anything terribly helpful. Do you know what I think?"

"I'd love to know," said Fergie, who had suddenly appeared in the doorway of the kitchen.

The professor smiled wryly. "I might have known you'd show up when food was cooking," he said. "As I was about to say when I was so rudely interrupted, I think the three of us ought to go on a camping expedition. This place is giving us all the willies, and there's nothing in Perry's will that says I have to stay here in the house every single blasted second during the summer. I hate to act as if I'm running away from a problem, but . . . well, it'd do us all a world of good to get away for at least one night. What do you say?"

Johnny and Fergie agreed enthusiastically, and so the camping trip was on. For the rest of the morning the boys stuffed clothing into their duffel bags, checked the batteries in their flashlights, and began loading camping equipment into the car. The professor cleaned the Coleman lamp and filled its fuel tank with kerosene. He drove into town and bought some bacon and beans and a couple of cans of Sterno for cooking out in the open. Then he fussed for about an hour, checking and rechecking his supplies and equipment and poring over road maps. Finally, around noon, he gathered the boys out on the front porch of the mansion and announced that they were ready to go.

"You'd think we were goin' to Mars, the way he's been actin'," muttered Fergie when he thought the professor's back was turned.

In a flash the professor whirled around. "What was that, Byron Ferguson?" he snapped.

Fergie's face got red. "Uh . . . I was just sayin' to John here that, uh, I was kind of wonderin' where exactly we were goin' to. I mean, you haven't told us yet."

The professor grinned and folded his arms. "No, I haven't told you, have I? Well, it's not exactly a state secret. We're going to drive up the road and rent a boat and put-put to an island in the middle of Lake Umbagog. It's a nice woodsy place and it actually is part of the estate, so we won't be trespassing. We can stay for a night or two, and I'll teach you two to fish, if you're willing to learn. Does that answer your questions?"

Fergie laughed, and then he and Johnny followed the professor out to the car, which was all packed and ready to go. They drove for about half an hour, until they pulled up next to a big barnlike building with a sagging roof. A square wooden board with MIKE FLYNN'S BOAT-HOUSE—BOATS FOR RENT painted on it in large sloppy black letters was propped against the side of the building. The boathouse stood on a small inlet that was part of Lake Umbagog, and down by the shore an old man was sitting on a stump and whittling a wooden duck decoy. When he heard the professor's car arrive, he glanced up in a bored way and then went on with his whittling. While the boys waited in the car, the professor got out and went to talk to the man. They argued for a fairly long time, and when the professor finally got back to the car he looked thoroughly crabby.

"Imagine the nerve of the old coot!" he grumbled, as he slid onto his seat. "Wanted to charge me because I'm leaving the car here for a day or two."

Johnny's heart sank. "Does—does that mean the trip is off?" he asked in a faltering voice.

"No, of course not!" snapped the professor. "I paid him what he wanted, so let's get our baggage out of the car and lug it down to the boat. Come on, gentlemen! Time's a-wasting!"

The boys helped the professor carry all the camping equipment down to the shore, and soon a rowboat with an outboard motor came drifting out of the boathouse. The old man nosed the boat over to the shore, got out, and stood watching as the campers loaded their stuff in. When everybody was aboard, the professor pulled the starting cord on the motor and they went putting across the water.

For a long time the boat skimmed along on the placid lake, as the wooded island got closer and closer. The boys jumped onto the sandy shore, tugging at the boat's prow while the professor started unloading things. When the boat was securely beached, they put up the tent in a flat, grassy space not far from the water and pounded stakes into the sandy earth. Then the boys stripped down to their bathing suits and ran into the water, while the professor sat on a folding stool under the tent's awning and puffed Balkan Sobranie cigarettes. Later they hopped into the boat and went fishing. The professor caught a walleyed pike, but he threw it back because the job of cleaning fish disgusted him. Since their fishing expedition wasn't turning out so well they decided to ride around the many islands that dotted the surface of the lake. Here and there they saw little cabins with screened porches and wondered whether anyone was staying in them. Sometimes a cabin looked utterly deserted, but others had boats tied up at their rickety docks.

When the three campers got back to their island, the sun was setting. Shadows deepened under the tall pines as the professor lit a canned-heat fire down by the beach and fried bacon in a skillet. He placed a portable grill over the fire and heated up beans and even made a pot of coffee. When dinner was over, Fergie got out his harmonica and played while the other two sang "Down in the Valley" and "Waltzing Matilda" and "Jolly, Jolly Sixpence." Twilight deepened, and the stars came out. The professor told stories about World War I and the strange people he had known in his life. Then they sang some more. They were all beginning to get sleepy. The professor yawned and said that he was going to turn in, but the boys decided that they would take a walk around the island before going to bed. By the time they got back to the tent they saw that the Coleman lamp was out, and the flaps were shut. From inside the tent came the gentle sound of snoring.

"Dead to the world," said Fergie with a grin. He looked thoughtfully out across the dark water. In the distance a tiny flickering light showed where Mike Flynn's boathouse was. Suddenly Fergie turned to Johnny. "Hey, John baby!" he whispered excitedly. "Let's borrow the boat an' go look at one of those islands we saw this afternoon. Whaddaya say?"

Johnny was flabbergasted. "Fergie," he whispered, "that is one of the dumbest ideas you have ever had! What if the professor wakes up and finds out that we're gone?"

"When we get back the prof will still be in dreamland," snapped Fergie. "Stop bein' such a worrywart!"

"The motor will wake him up," said Johnny stubbornly.

"So we'll use the oars," Fergie shot back. "They don't hardly make any noise at all."

Johnny was startled. He glanced down toward the water, and sure enough, there were two oars fastened to brackets on the sides of the boat. Biting his lip, Johnny paced up and down for a few seconds. "Oh, all *right*!" he said finally as he turned to face Fergie. "But if we get into trouble it's gonna be all your fault!"

Fergie shrugged carelessly and started walking down to the shore. With Johnny's help he got the boat into the water, and then he pulled the oars out of the brackets and fitted the oarlocks into their holes. Johnny sat in the rear and tried to act calm and confident, though his nerves were very much on edge. Swiftly they glided away, with no sound but the gentle slosh of the oar blades as they hit the water. Fergie hummed "Row, Row, Row Your Boat" and Johnny joined in, singing quietly. Soon they were among the tiny islands they had visited earlier in the day. A few cabin windows were lit, and they could hear laughing and the slamming of screen doors and the sound of radios playing. Fergie was steering toward a little island that sat all by itself, a long way from the others. As they pulled closer to it, Johnny began to feel afraid. A tight knot formed in his stomach and the palms of his hands felt sweaty.

"Fergie?" he asked in a trembling voice. "Are . . . I mean, do you feel anything strange?"

Fergie grinned. "Nope. You musta had too much of the prof's cooking." Actually, Fergie was lying. He felt nervous too, but he would never have admitted it to Johnny.

As they glided closer they could see a weak yellowish light shining in the window of a cottage on the island. A kerosene lamp, probably. A rickety dock reached out from the shore into the water, but no boat was tied up to it.

"Hey!" exclaimed Fergie delightedly. "How about that, eh? The people must be gone, so we can go in an' have a look-see. Just for a minute and then we'll leave. Okay?"

Johnny felt alarmed. He was normally a very law-abiding boy, and he didn't much like the idea of trespassing. But he knew with a sinking heart that he was going to keep his mouth shut and let Fergie lead him into trouble, because he did not want Fergie to call him chicken.

Expertly Fergie maneuvered the boat in toward the dock, and he grabbed a mossy post and held it while Johnny slipped a loop of rope over the end. As quietly as possible they clambered up onto the dock and padded toward the shore. Ducking in under some pine branches, the two boys followed a sandy path up toward the screened porch of the little cottage. The path turned right and wound past one side of the cottage, and the boys followed it till they came to a small lighted window. The window was too high for peeking, but after glancing around, Fergie found an old soda-bottle crate and set it under the window. He climbed up and peered in, and then he let out a long low whistle.

"Hey, John baby!" he whispered. "Get a load of this! This joint must belong to that strange character we bumped into on the street the other day! Come on up and look!"

There was room on the crate for two people, and after hesitating a bit Johnny climbed up and peered in. He saw a room with knotty-pine paneling, a fieldstone fireplace, and an old ratty sofa with the stuffing coming out of the arms. In the middle of the bare floor stood a well-scrubbed wooden table with a cane-bottomed chair facing it. On the table stood a kerosene lamp and a collection of ivory chessmen. They looked just like the ones that had spilled from the leather case after the professor bumped into the strange man in the British overcoat.

"My gosh!" Johnny whispered in an awestruck voice. "What do you think that guy is doin' out here?"

"Playin' chess without a chessboard," Fergie muttered with a laugh. "An' there's somethin' that looks like a chart on the table. I wonder if I can see what it is."

Putting his hands on the grimy windowsill and rising up on tiptoe, Fergie craned his neck and looked. With a little puzzled snort he lowered himself back down. "Huh! That's funny!"

"What's funny?" asked Johnny nervously.

"Well, it's a chart of the heavens. You know, with

stars and planets and constellations—that's what it looks like, anyway. I said that guy was a fruitcake, didn't I? Well, this sort of proves it!"

Johnny said nothing. He found that he was getting more and more jumpy by the minute. Suppose that the man came back and found them here? Grabbing Fergie by the arm, he began to plead. "Come on! Let's get away from this place before something awful happens! I can't tell you why, but I feel like there's somebody here watching us!"

Fergie was about to exclaim that that was the dumbest piece of nervous nonsense he had ever heard of, when a harsh, grating voice behind them said, "Good evening, boys! And what do you think *you're* doing?"

CHAPTER SEVEN

Johnny's blood froze, and Fergie stiffened. Slowly the two boys turned around, and they found that they were staring at the nasty ruddy-faced man with the pointed mustache and the British accent. A halo of greenish light hovered about the man, and when he raised his hand, Johnny and Fergie found that they could not speak or move.

"What charming visitors you are!" sneered the man, as he stepped closer. "Of course, you did drop in un-invited, so you'll have to take the consequences. *Down on your knees, both of you! At once!*"

Awkwardly Johnny and Fergie stumbled down off the box and knelt before the evilly grinning man. After a brief pause the man stooped and put his hand under Johnny's chin. He jerked the boy's head upward.

"Now, then, you little wretch, listen to me and listen carefully!" snarled the man. "I could kill you both so easily, but I'd rather not do that—not just yet. You two will die along with the rest. The earth will be a smoldering ball of rubble then, but I will survive as a spirit with heightened consciousness and great power. But why should I spend my time explaining things to morons? You'll see the face of doom in a very short while, and I want you to know that there's nothing—absolutely nothing—that you can do to stop me. As for that doddering old fool, that professor friend of yours . . . well, he isn't as smart as he thinks he is. No one can keep me from my destiny! *No one!*" He raised his hand in the air imperiously. "And now I am finished with you," he intoned, in a haughty voice. "When you go back you will not remember that we've met. You will not remember anything that I have said. *In nomine Tetragrammaton*, depart! Go back with fear in your hearts and blankness in your minds! *Vade in perditionem!* Begone, I charge ye, by the names of the twelve living spirits that stand by the throne of the Prince of the Air! *Go!*"

The man clapped his hands twice, and his body seemed to melt into the shadows under the trees that grew close to the cottage. A full minute passed, and then Johnny and Fergie slowly pulled themselves to their feet. Johnny's neck ached, and he felt dizzy. He turned to look at Fergie, who was still acting woozy and shaking his head, like someone who has just been awakened out of a sound sleep.

"What—what happened?" asked Johnny in a thick, groggy voice. He could not figure out why the two of them had been on their knees, facing away from the cottage.

Fergie rubbed his hands over his face. "John baby," he said slowly, "if I knew what happened, I'd tell you. Somebody must've hit us on the head—that's the only explanation I can come up with. But who did it? And how come my head doesn't hurt?"

Johnny paused and looked around at the dark, menacing shadows of the trees. "I think we better get out of here," he said in a worried voice. "We might get murdered if we hang around much longer."

Fergie did not need any more encouragement. He grabbed Johnny by the arm and shoved him ahead and soon they were trotting along, double time, toward the dock and the boat that still bobbed on the choppy water. Quickly they piled in, and Fergie seized the oars. Johnny pulled the rope free of the post, and they glided away, driven by Fergie's strong strokes. The dark shadow of the island got smaller and smaller, and the fear that had gripped them melted away. But neither said anything. They both knew that they had had a strange and frightening experience, and they were still struggling with their feelings. There was a blank spot in their lives, time they couldn't account for, and this bothered them very much.

Back across the lake water they slid. Fergie rowed grimly on, and Johnny glanced absentmindedly about. Then he happened to look up at the starry sky. Suddenly he let out a sharp, loud exclamation.

"My gosh, Fergie! *Look!*"

"Huh? Look at what?"

"Up overhead! In the sky!"

Fergie looked, and his mouth dropped open. A bright, long-tailed comet was burning in the sky. "Holy Toledo!" he gasped. "How about that! I didn't know there was one of those comin' our way, did you?"

"We wouldn't have known about it," said Johnny sourly. "The professor keeps turning off the TV news at night because it depresses him, and we aren't getting any newspapers." He bent his head back and stared some more. "That really is something, isn't it?" he went on in an awestruck tone. "I've never seen one before, have you?"

Fergie shook his head. "Nope. Well, now I guess I've seen everything! We'll have to tell the prof about this when he wakes up."

"If he isn't already waiting for us down by the shore," said Johnny gloomily.

When they got back to the island where they were camping, Johnny and Fergie were relieved to see that the tent was dark and still, with its flaps tied shut. Carefully Fergie nosed the boat in, and then he and Johnny dragged it up onto the sand as quietly as they could. They put the oars in the brackets and tiptoed back to the tent, lifted the flaps, and crawled inside. Their sleeping bags were ready for them, and the professor was in his, snoring peacefully. The little nighttime adventure had turned strange, but they were lucky to have returned safely.

The next morning, as they were eating breakfast, Johnny cautiously brought up the subject of the comet. "Uh . . . professor? You know what?"

The professor swallowed a mouthful of eggs and turned to Johnny. "No, I don't have the slightest idea what, John," he said, grinning. "Tell me what."

Johnny squirmed. He was afraid he might accidentally tell the professor where they had been last night, and this made him jittery. "I . . . uh, well, Fergie and I were sitting up late last night after you went to bed, and—and we saw a comet!"

The professor nodded knowingly. "Yes, I knew that there was one on the way. I read about it in a newspaper at the library the other day. And for your information, there are two more coming, though they won't be visible till later this summer. The astronomers are all worked up because we haven't had so many comets in . . . well, a very long time. I'm an old geezer, so I remember Halley's Comet in 1910, but I'll bet neither of you has ever seen one before. Have you?"

Fergie and Johnny shook their heads. Then an odd thought came to Johnny. "Professor," he asked with a hint of nervousness in his voice, "what do you think is causing all these comets to show up?"

The professor shrugged. "Search me, John! I'm no expert on these things, but if I had to guess I'd say that there was a disturbance in the Oort cloud."

Fergie blinked. "The *what?*"

The professor smiled complacently. "Got you with that one, didn't I? The Oort cloud is just a theory dreamed up in 1950 by a Dutch astronomer named Oort. He thinks that there is a whole mess of comets orbiting the solar system, way out beyond the farthest planet. According to his idea every now and then some asteroid or meteor plows into the Oort cloud, jars some of these comets loose, and sends them streaking toward the sun. At one time, by the way, comets were regarded as evil omens. But we know that's nonsense now. Comets are just a natural phenomenon, nothing more."

Johnny smiled weakly and felt his stomach turn over. He thought about the chart of the heavens that he had seen in the cottage. A vague fear began to form in his mind. "These—these comets couldn't hit the earth, could they?" he asked in a trembling voice.

The professor stared at Johnny for a second, and then he laughed loudly. "Good heavens, John!" he exclaimed. "What sort of science-fiction nonsense have you been reading lately? Comets may have hit the earth ages and ages ago, but it's not the sort of thing that happens anymore! Rest easy, we're not going to be blitzed by comets. When they pass the earth, they're usually millions of miles away, and then they zoom around the sun and go back into outer space. Whatever made you ask a question like that?"

Johnny stared at his plate. "I—I don't know," he mumbled. "Maybe it was something I read about."

"Well, you should read other things!" said the professor brusquely. "And now, if you two are through feeding your faces, I would like you to help me wash these dirty dishes and pack our things before we head back to the estate. Hop to it, gentlemen!"

Fergie and Johnny helped the professor take down the tent and clean up the campsite. They packed up their equipment and put-putted back to Mike Flynn's boathouse. As they drove to the estate, the half-memory of the strange incident on the Englishman's island kept flitting back into Johnny's brain. It was a maddening feeling, and Johnny would have enjoyed talking with Fergie about it. But he knew from the look on Fergie's face that he was going to clam up and pretend to be a tough guy. He would act as if the incident had never happened.

Weeks passed. August arrived, and the Perseid meteor showers appeared in the sky, as they always do. Along with the meteors came the two comets that the professor had told the boys about. Each night the comets burned like lamps in the sky, side by side. A lot of articles were written in the newspapers about this incredible celestial event and nutty letters saying doom was near appeared in the "Letters to the Editor" columns all across the country. The professor laughed whenever he heard of things like this, but Johnny and Fergie were not as skeptical as he was. They felt nervous and tense, and they wondered what was going to happen.

One hot muggy evening in the middle of August, Johnny, Fergie, and the professor were driving back from a visit to Stone Arabia. They had seen a movie and gobbled Big Ed's wonderful chiliburgers, and they were in a very good mood, singing songs and telling jokes. When they rounded the last turn of the driveway they were surprised to see that the old mansion was ablaze with light. Every window was glowing, except for the boarded windows in the room on the third story of the tower. But even there, through the cracks, faint glimmers of light could be seen.

"Great God in heaven!" exclaimed the professor as he jammed on the brakes and shut the motor off. "It looks as if someone has been having a party here while we were gone! What do you think we should do? Drive back to town and get the police?"

Fergie shook his head. "Naah, Prof," he muttered through his teeth. "It looks like some old bum has broken in an' is havin' a high old time. I think the three of us can handle him."

At first the professor wanted to tell Fergie that he was out of his mind. But then he remembered the time he had charged a machine-gun nest, single handed, during the battle of the Argonne Forest. He pulled himself together and set his jaw. "No doubt you are right, Byron," he said stiffly. "Are you with me, gentlemen? Then it's forward at a gallop!"

Secretly Johnny wished that his two friends were not so bold and fearless. But on the other hand he didn't want anyone to accuse him of being a coward, so he slid off his seat and followed Fergie and the professor up the sidewalk toward the mansion. The professor led the way, with a tire iron gripped firmly in his right hand. But about halfway up the walk he stopped. He tried to go on, but he couldn't—he had run into an invisible wall that was as solid as the side of a mountain. With an astonished look on his face the professor stepped backward. He gritted his teeth and strode forward again, but he was stopped so suddenly that his glasses were knocked askew. With a muttered curse the professor took two steps back and adjusted his spectacles. Then he turned to the boys, who were standing and watching with their mouths open.

"Gentlemen," he growled in a low, angry voice, "it seems that we are up against something that is stronger than us. If we were smart, I suppose we would skedaddle out of here. But I want to know what's going on. Are you with me?"

The boys nodded and folded their arms stubbornly. Minutes passed, as they stood waiting outside the strange invisible wall that encircled the huge old house. Ahead they could see the lights still burning. Overhead, in the night sky, the two strange comets raced along, with fiery tails streaming behind them. For about half an hour nothing happened. Johnny thought that he heard a distant sound of chanting coming from the boarded room in the tower, but the sound was so faint that he could not tell if it was real. The professor got more and more nervous, and he paced back and forth.

"What on earth time is it?" snapped the professor irritably. "I left my watch in the house. Do you have a timepiece, Byron?"

Fergie squinted at the luminous dial of his watch. "I think it's about midnight, Prof," he said. "This thing isn't terribly accurate, but I set it this morning so it's probably right."

The professor scowled and folded his arms. "Ah, midnight! The witching hour! Traditionally this is the time when all sorts of weird and uncanny things are likely to occur. I wonder if—"

At that moment a loud slamming split the air. It sounded like a heavy load of wooden planks being dropped from a great height. At the same instant all the lights in the mansion went out, and the earth shook. It shook so violently that the professor and the boys were thrown to their knees. Dazed and shaken, Johnny tried to drag himself to his feet, but he found that he couldn't. For some reason he bent his head backward and gazed up at the two bright comets that still streaked across the heavens. As he watched, the comets seemed to flicker and grow dim. Then they went out. They vanished, and only the vast starry gulf of the night sky could be seen.

CHAPTER EIGHT

Something incredible had happened. For a long time
the professor and the boys knelt motionless on the damp
grass, but finally, one by one, they pulled themselves to
their feet. Johnny looked up at the sky where no comets
burned; he looked at the dark house that was lost in the
shadows of night. Had they all been dreaming? How
could burning comets vanish? How could an invisible
wall keep them out of their house? Clutching his arms
to his sides, he shuddered and closed his eyes. When he
opened them he saw the professor brushing grass off his
pants. When the professor saw that Johnny was staring
at him, he straightened up and pushed his glasses straight
on his nose.

"Well, that was something, wasn't it?" he snorted, as

he looked around. "Byron, are you all right?"

Fergie was standing nearby. He seemed stunned, but when he spoke, his voice was clear and reassuring. "I guess so, Prof," he said as he ran his hands over his arms. "No bones broken, but . . . hey, what do you think happened? I mean, comets don't just go out, do they?"

The professor shook his head firmly. "No, they assuredly do not! You can be sure that astronomers all over the world will be having a field day with this one! But come, gentlemen ! Let us see if we can get into our house."

Stepping forward, the professor groped with his hands, but he felt nothing—nothing but air. Beckoning to the boys, he led the way up the walk to the wide pillared porch. But when he jerked open the front door and turned on the hall light, he got a rude surprise. The house looked as if a whirlwind had passed through it. Pictures had fallen off the walls, and the coat tree had fallen on its face. Mirrors were shattered, and table lamps had been flung about. The professor stalked from room to room with the boys close behind him, and they all stared in disbelief at the mess in every part of the house.

"Lord preserve us!" sighed the professor, as he paused to catch his breath. "I'll bet the creep who did this has a red beefy face and a waxed mustache. Boys, will you come with me to the tower room?"

Johnny and Fergie glanced quickly at each other. They felt scared, but they also felt angry and determined.

"We're with you, Prof!" said Fergie loudly. "Lead on!"

Without another word the professor led the way up the main staircase, along the upstairs hall, and up the narrow, creaky flight of steps that mounted to the tower room. The three of them paused for a long time outside the stout paneled door, but at last the professor summoned up his courage and stepped forward. Shoving the door open, he groped for the light switch and flipped it on. After a brief hesitation the boys followed the professor inside, and they glanced curiously around at the ugly deserted room. All was still, and an unpleasant burnt smell hung in the air. The professor looked around, and then with a muttered curse he rushed to the fireplace. Standing up on tiptoe and gripping the mantel with his fingers, he peered hard at the metal disk that covered the stovepipe hole in the chimney. With amazement the professor saw that the pretty painted scene of trees and flowers had been scraped away, and now it was clear that the disk was not made of metal at all—it was transparent, like window glass! With a sudden lunge the professor rose up on tiptoe and banged on the disk with his fist. Something fell onto the fireplace hearth with a loud hollow *clack!* "By God!" said the professor. Fergie and Johnny gasped. Between the brass andirons lay a charred human skull with long black hair.

In an instant the professor was on his knees. He reached into the fireplace, grabbed the skull, and held it up for the boys to see. A wild light was in his eyes.

"This is it!" he exclaimed triumphantly as he tapped

one of the hollow eye sockets with his finger. "A dead eye in a room with no view! That evil mustached wretch was here tonight, trying to work black magic. And I think he almost succeeded!"

Johnny and Fergie were stunned. What on earth was the professor saying?

"I—I don't quite get you, Prof," said Fergie with a quick, nervous glance at Johnny. "What do you mean?"

The professor pulled himself to his feet. The grisly charred skull was still in his hands. "I mean," he said quietly, "that a magic ritual was performed here, and I think that it had something to do with those two comets. I know it sounds incredible, but . . . look, let's go downstairs. This evil room is giving me the screaming woo-hoos!"

Holding the skull at arm's length, the professor put it inside the closet. Then he led the boys downstairs to the kitchen, where they all got glasses of lemonade.

Slowly and solemnly they went out to the porch and sat down on three cane-bottomed rockers. The crickets chirped loudly in the tall grass, and the stars burned brightly in the sky. For a long time no one said anything. Finally the professor broke the silence.

"As I was going to say earlier," he muttered in a dreamy, faraway voice, "I think the last piece of the puzzle has fallen into place. Remember the end of my brother's weird poem? He talks about dragging the hairy stars from their nest. Well, it just came to me a few minutes ago that comets are hairy stars. That is what the ancient Greeks called them, because they thought that the long streaming tails were like hair. And the nest of comets is the Oort cloud that I was telling you about earlier. Somehow that evil man is using those chessmen and some occult ceremonies to bring comets toward the earth. But does he just want to scare people, or does he have something far more vicious in mind? He seems to be carrying out some project that was begun by my dear dead brother. I'd give a lot to know what our nasty friend really has in mind. But we may not know that until it's too late."

Johnny and Fergie looked at each other anxiously. Could the professor be right? Could the man with the chessmen really control comets? It seemed unlikely, but then a lot of unlikely things had been happening around Perry's old estate in the last two months. Silence fell. The only sounds were the chirping of the crickets and the creaking of the rockers. Suddenly Johnny spoke up.

"Uh . . . Professor?" he said, in a weak, throaty voice. "I have something to tell you. That is, we do. We—I mean, Fergie and me—we sneaked out with the boat on the night we were camping on that island, and—and we saw that nasty guy's cabin and the chessmen."

The professor was shocked. For a while he said nothing, and when he finally spoke his voice was strained—he was trying hard to keep from exploding.

"I see," he said through his teeth. "Would you care to tell me any more about your nocturnal adventure?"

With a lot of hems and haws, Johnny told the story of their trip to the evil man's island. And he tried to explain, as well as he could, the weird blanked-out feeling that he and Fergie had had after their visit. The professor listened intently, and when Johnny was through he heaved a deep discontented sigh and rubbed his hands over his face.

"I wish I could get angry with you boys," he said, "but I always enjoyed going on nighttime adventures when I was a kid, and some of them were a bit hair-raising. Hmph! So you saw the nasty man's cottage, the chessmen, and a chart of the heavens. That certainly fits in with what I've managed to figure out. But the question now is: What do we do?"

"We could swipe those chessmen from him," suggested Fergie. "Without them, he can't do his magic whoop-te-doo, can he?"

The professor eyed Fergie coldly. "Oh, that's just a great big wonderful idea," he said. "Here we have someone who can keep us out of our house with an invisible wall, and we're supposed to sneak up on him and grab the chessmen while he's taking a nap?"

"We could swipe them while he's away somewhere," said Fergie stubbornly. "He has to eat like ordinary people, doesn't he? Well, maybe when he's gone into town for some food we can creep up in a rowboat. It might not work, but we oughta give it a try. It's better than not doing *anything*!"

The professor put his glass of lemonade down on the floor of the porch. Then he folded his arms and rocked for a while in silence.

"You know, Byron," he said slowly, "there are times when you show signs of intelligence. The filthy wretch has to leave his silly island *sometime*! Of course, he may take the chessmen with him when he goes, but there's always the chance that he'll leave them at the cabin the way he did the night you two paid your visit. We should find out where he gets his supplies. It'll probably be at the general store in Stone Arabia, because it's close to the lake. I'll get friendly with the owner and see if I can get him to tell me when Uglypuss usually comes to town. Then we can borrow a motorboat and go zipping on out to the island. How does that sound?"

Johnny tried to smile, but he just couldn't manage it. He thought the plan was crummy, and he also thought that Fergie and the professor were out of their minds for suggesting it. However, he knew that he would have to go along, because the other two were exceptionally strong-willed people. If something went wrong, they would all get killed together.

Days passed, and the professor laid the groundwork for his plan. He got into a friendly checker game with Mr. Blodgett, the owner of the general store in Stone Arabia, and managed to find out that the nasty man was named Edmund Stallybrass, and he was a man of very regular habits. Every Monday afternoon he came into town for supplies, and he spent the evening playing cards in the back room of a local tavern. He never went home till ten or eleven o'clock. So, on the very next Monday afternoon, around four o'clock, the professor set out to rent another motorboat. He had decided that Mike Flynn's prices were too high, so he went to another boathouse about a quarter of the way around the lake from Mr. Flynn's place. Rain was falling and the wind was whistling in the trees as the professor's car jolted down the muddy track that led to Higbee's Landing. The professor was wearing his yellow slicker and black rubber rain hat, and he was in high spirits. The boys wore plastic raincoats and were hatless. Both smiled bravely, but inside they were very tense—their stomachs were knotted up with fear. The professor guessed the boys' thoughts, and he tried to cheer them up.

"Come, gentlemen!" he said jauntily. "Banish dull care and worry! This is going to be a breeze! Out to the island we go, we snatch old Nasty's chessmen, and back we come. Easy as pie!"

"Yeah. Right you are, Prof," muttered Fergie without enthusiasm. He had been having second thoughts about this expedition lately, and it wouldn't have taken much talking to make him decide to stay home.

"We're with you all the way," said Johnny tonelessly. At present he was wishing that he were back in Duston Heights.

"Thank you both for your enthusiastic support," said the professor. "I can go by myself, if you wish."

Johnny opened his mouth to say that he wouldn't mind

staying behind, but then he saw Fergie's grim expression. If anyone suggested that Fergie was a coward, he would plunge headlong into an adventure, no matter how dangerous it was.

"I'm not stayin' home!" said Fergie stubbornly. "An' neither is John—are you, John baby?"

Johnny shook his head and stared dully at the wagging windshield wipers. He was in up to his neck, whether he wanted to be or not.

The boys waited in the car while the professor talked to Mr. Higbee. Soon he came back, all smiles and good humor. It turned out that he had gotten a better deal from Mr. Higbee than he had gotten from Mike Flynn. So the boys piled out of the car and followed the professor down to the sagging dock, where a small white boat with an Evinrude outboard motor waited. The boys climbed in while the professor settled himself in the stern and adjusted the spark of the engine. With a grand flourish he pulled the cord, and a loud droning sound began. With an excited gleam in his eye the professor began to sing "The Skye Boat Song." It was about the time the future King Charles II of England was taken by fishing boat to the lonely Isle of Skye so that his enemies would not be able to seize him. Johnny knew the words too, and he sang along:

> Speed, bonny boat, like a bird on the wing
> Onward! the sailors cry;
> Carry the lad that's born to be king
> Over the sea to Skye. . . .

It was still raining. The distant islands were hidden by mist, and Johnny began to worry about rainwater filling up the boat. A rusty tomato can lay at his feet, but it would not be much use if they really had to bail. And there were other worries on his mind too.

"Do you think we can find the island in all this rain?" he asked. Johnny had to cup his hands to his mouth and yell, because of the roaring motor.

"I think I know where it is," the professor shouted back. "It's just beyond those islands up ahead!"

What islands? thought Johnny. All he could see beyond the boat's prow were blowing shawls of gray murk. The weather began to get worse. The wind whipped into a gale, and sheets of rain slapped at their faces, soaking them. The professor gritted his teeth, and it was almost as if he were forcing the boat forward by the power of his will. Suddenly, with a jarring *crrunch*! the boat stopped. They had run aground.

"Well, isn't this nice!" growled the professor. "I wonder where the devil we are!"

It was hard to tell. Through the mist and rain they could see the vague shapes of swaying pine trees, but that was about all. This might be Mr. Stallybrass's island, or it might not. Rain pattered on the bottom of the boat and the wind made an eerie keening sound as it whipped the pine boughs. Finally the professor forced himself to his feet. He clambered over the side into water that was only up to his ankles. Johnny and Fergie got out too, and they dragged the boat farther onto the gravelly beach. The professor unhooked the khaki-colored Boy Scout flashlight from his belt and turned it on. Slowly, hesitantly, he began to pick his way up the beach, and the boys followed him. Suddenly they stopped. A bell was ringing, a high-pitched clangy bell.

"What is *that*?" exclaimed the professor as he squinted into the mist. "Do you remember if there was a dinner bell on Stallybrass's island?"

Fergie shrugged. "We didn't see any, Prof, but it was dark. There might've been one, for all I know."

Johnny said that he had seen a big bronze bell mounted in a tree, but it was on one of the large islands that they had passed during their daytime cruise.

"Fine!" grumped the professor, as he folded his arms in disgust. "Someone is probably ringing the bell in alarm because there are trespassers on their island. With luck, we'll have German shepherd dogs chewing at our ankles in a few minutes." He heaved a deep, discontented sigh. "Well, gentlemen," he went on, "there's no point in sailing in that storm, so we'll just have to throw ourselves on the mercy of whoever lives here. I think I see a path among those trees over there—let's go and show them that we mean no harm."

With the boys close behind him the professor stomped up the beach and onto the winding sandy path. The bell clanged on. Finally, through the mist, they saw a glimmering yellow light. Cheered up by this sign of life, the three travelers walked faster. At last they came into a clearing and saw a small stone chapel with a stubby bell tower. Lights were on in the chapel, and the door was open.

The boys and the professor halted. They stared in wonder at this strange building and they felt afraid. Why was there a chapel way out here on an island, and why was it lit up in the middle of the night? Why was the bell ringing? The professor looked at the boys. Johnny wanted to run back to the boat, but with a mighty effort of will he forced himself to stay where he was. Fergie grew tense and groped in his pocket for the switchblade knife he always carried.

"I don't suppose there's any point in standing out here forever," said the professor in a tight strained voice. "So let us go in and see for whom the bell tolls." With that he clenched his hand around his flashlight and stepped resolutely forward.

As they crossed the threshold, the boys and the professor looked warily around. The chapel was empty. Rows of varnished pews stretched toward the communion rail, and on the altar six tall candles burned. Before the rail three coffins stood on sawhorses. A black woollen pall with a white cross was draped over each. A faint smell of incense and candle wax hung in the air.

Silently the professor began walking down the aisle, and the boys followed him. They paused briefly by the coffins and then went up three broad steps and through the gate in the railing. They stood in the sanctuary, glancing about nervously. The bell had stopped clanging, and the silence seemed deafening. Johnny felt a chill creeping over his body. He looked at the other two, and from their pale, tense faces he knew that they felt the way he did. At last, after what seemed like forever, the professor spoke.

"All this is very odd indeed," he muttered in a voice that trembled a bit. "Here we have everything ready for a funeral—a multiple funeral, it seems—and yet there are no mourners, no priests or ministers, no. . ."

His voice died. A small door on the right side of the sanctuary had opened noiselessly, and a man in a long black cassock walked into the room. His hands were pale and bony, and his face reminded Johnny of a skull. His red-rimmed eyes burned in deep-set sockets. As they watched, this strange-looking man crossed the polished floor, nodded quickly toward the crucifix on the altar, and walked over to where they were standing.

"Good evening," he said in an odd, high-pitched voice. "Can I be of any assistance to you?"

The professor waited about half a minute before speaking. A lot of weird thoughts were running through his mind, and none of them were very pleasant.

"I was wondering," he said at last, "if there is a funeral that is going to take place here."

The man grinned unpleasantly. "You are very perceptive," he said in a mocking tone. "Very perceptive indeed. We are here to mourn the passing of three vacationers—two boys and an old man—who died tragically in a boating accident. If you wish to stay for the funeral service, you may."

The words of this strange man struck terror into the hearts of the boys and the professor. Panic rose inside them, and they began to wonder if they had gotten trapped inside a nightmare. After a wild look around, the professor dashed to the three coffins. With a quick twist of his hand he flicked the pall away from one, and peered at the brass plate that was bolted to the mahogany lid. The engraved letters seemed to squirm before his eyes:

In memory of

RODERICK CHILDERMASS

tragically drowned

in

Lake Umbagog

R.I.P.

With a wild, frightened yell the professor whirled around. The man was gone. Johnny and Fergie stood staring at the coffins, their eyes wide with fear.

"Where is he?" barked the professor. "Where the devil has he gone to?"

"He . . . just disappeared," said Johnny in a small, throaty voice. "Professor, what's going on?"

Frightened, the professor grabbed Johnny's arm. *"Come on, you two!"* he yelled. *"We've got to get out of here!"*

The boys didn't need to be persuaded. Madly they pounded down the aisle after the professor, and before they knew it they were on the path, with the wind blowing rain in their faces. They tripped over logs and roots in their haste to escape. Gasping for breath, they finally arrived at the shore, where the rented boat waited. It had been raining so hard that there was a lot of water in the bottom of the boat, but that did not matter. Johnny and Fergie threw their weight against the bow, and the boat slid into the choppy, rain-swept lake. Splashing through the surf, the professor clambered into the boat and tried to start the engine. On the first three tries nothing happened. He tore open the engine's hood and took out the spark plugs. After drying them hastily with his handkerchief he put them back and once more pulled at the starting cord. The Evinrude engine roared into life, and the boat sped out onto the lake. Clinging to the gunwales with their hands, the boys cheered wildly, because it looked as if their troubles were over. But all of a sudden the outboard engine coughed, sputtered, and died. Angrily the professor jerked at the cord, but it was no use. The wind buffeted the boat, slapping it this way and that. The water in the bottom rose to ankle level, and Johnny dropped to his knees and began frantically bailing with the tomato can. "O God, our refuge and our strength," he prayed, saying the same phrase over and over, but his words were whipped away by the howling wind. The boat heeled to the wind, drifting helplessly, and then suddenly Fergie stood up. A wild, frightened light was in his eyes.

"*We're all gonna die!*" he screamed, waving his arms "*Help us, somebody! Please help!*"

"Sit down!" bellowed the professor with his hands

cupped to his mouth. "For heaven's sake, sit down or you'll—"

He never got to finish his sentence. With wild wind-milling gestures Fergie lurched to one side. The boat rocked dangerously and then tipped over, and all three were plunged into the cold, churning waters of the lake.

CHAPTER NINE

As the gray drizzly morning dawned, three very wet and bedraggled figures sat perched on an overturned rowboat. Johnny was at one end, Fergie was at the other, and the professor crouched in the middle, with the canoe paddle in his hand. His hair was sopping wet and was plastered to his forehead, and there was a very crabby expression on his face.

"I feel absolutely wretched," growled the old man. "On the other hand, we are still alive, so I guess we ought to be grateful for small favors. How are you boys doing?"

"Pretty well, Prof," said Fergie wearily. "I'll bet you didn't know that a rowboat can hold more people upside down than it can right side up. I read that somewhere."

"I'll file that little piece of information away," said the professor dryly. He twisted his head around and peered at Johnny, who was straddling the stern of the boat. "How about you, John?"

Johnny felt waves of nausea rising inside him, but he fought them down, swallowed hard, and stared straight ahead. "I think I can hang on for a long time," he said bravely. "As long as there aren't any big waves, I mean. Do you suppose anyone will come to rescue us?"

As if in answer a droning motorboat sound began in the distance. It drew closer, and then a white-and-blue official-looking speedboat appeared out of the mist. A big swiveling searchlight was mounted on the front, and the words STONE ARABIA POLICE DEPT. were stenciled neatly on the side, under a silver star. A cop in a rain slicker stood in the bow, and he held a megaphone in his hand.

"Do you need help?" he bellowed.

The professor couldn't help laughing. "That must be one of the most idiotic questions I have ever heard in my life," he said between cackles. "Does it look like we're on a boating expedition?" he yelled back. "Yes, of course we need help!"

The police boat pulled alongside the upside-down rowboat and its three soaked occupants. One at a time the boys and the professor were pulled into the other vessel. Gratefully they sank onto the ribbed bottom.

"Many thanks, officer," sighed the professor. "I am very happy to see you!"

The policeman with the megaphone handed out blankets to the three wet and shivering people that he had rescued. Then the police boat did a very neat U-turn and went plowing away at high speed toward the shore.

That evening the professor and the boys were sitting in the study of the old mansion. A roaring fire was going in the fireplace, and everyone had a mug of hot cider in his hand. The boys looked dejected, while the professor looked mad enough to chew nails. For a long time there was no sound but the ticking of the gloomy black marble clock on the mantel and the crackling of twigs in the fireplace. Finally the professor spoke.

"Well, it was a nice try," he said sourly. "But I guess I should have expected that the Mustache Monster would beat us to the punch. He probably guessed what we would try to do and conjured up that chapel illusion, and threw in the storm for good measure. I have heard tales of sorcerers who could command the winds and the waves, but I never believed it until now."

Fergie made a squinchy face and stared into the fire. He was trying hard to be skeptical. "Are you sure that storm was his doing?" he asked with a sudden searching glance at the professor. "I mean, it could've been a coincidence, couldn't it?"

The professor stiffened. "Oh, sure!" he said in a strained voice. "That storm was a mere coincidence! It was also a coincidence that those comets in the sky went out during the magic ceremony that our friend was trying to perform here in the tower room of the mansion. Look,

Byron! I am as confused as you are about the things that have been going on around here lately. But I can tell you one thing: Dear Mr. Stallybrass may be as batty as a bedbug, but he has a lot of power and he's not shy about using it. Those lights in the sky may or may not have been comets. The storm may or may not have been summoned up by witchcraft. But *something* is going on, and it is evil. For that reason I think we are in great danger as long as we stay here. We have been up to bat twice against Mr. Stallybrass, and each time we have struck out. I think we had better escape while we still can."

Johnny's jaw dropped. He put his cider mug on the coffee table and stared at the professor. "You mean you're going to just go home?" he asked in amazement.

The professor nodded. "Yes, that is exactly what I am going to do. And you two are going with me because you really have no choice in the matter. I hate to sound like a tyrant, but I'm doing this for your good and for mine. We're like a bunch of people who are trying to put out a forest fire with water pistols—the chances of success are pretty slim."

Johnny and Fergie looked quickly at each other. Each one knew what the other was thinking—the professor really had not given up. He probably had some secret plan for settling Mr. Stallybrass's hash, but he wanted to protect the boys, so he was pretending to give up. Luckily the professor did not notice the looks the boys were giving each other—he was too busy trying to light an old meerschaum pipe that he had found in Perry's desk.

Johnny took a sip of cider and paused to let the warmth flow into his body. "Are—are you gonna give up the inheritance?" he asked hesitantly. He knew that the professor had to stay at the estate until Labor Day to collect the ten million dollars Perry had left him.

"Inheritance, shminheritance!" said the professor with a shrug. "I have enough money to last me the rest of my life, so I don't need to be greedy. I had hoped that I could use some of that dough to provide for your college education, John, but . . . well, I'd rather make sure that you and Byron stay among the living. Don't lose any sleep over the lost money. It probably had a curse on it anyway!"

The boys and the professor talked on until they were so weary that they saw spots dancing in front of their eyes. Then they gulped the last of their cider, turned out the lights in the study, and dragged themselves upstairs to their beds. In spite of the frightening adventure that they had had, they all slept soundly.

On a chilly sunlit day in August the three travelers said good-bye to the estate of Stone Arabia and its haunted tower room. A hint of fall was in the air, and red maple leaves sifted down onto the porch as the professor turned the key in the lock of the wide front door. The boys stood beside him, and the professor's maroon Pontiac waited in the driveway. Its trunk and

backseat were crammed with camping equipment, bed-
ding, canned goods, and other odds and ends. For a
long time the professor stood before the locked door with
his arms folded. He was trying to remember if he had
done everything that was necessary for shutting the house
down. There's always something that you forget to do,
said a little voice in the back of his head, but right now
he was not terribly interested in little nagging voices.
He wanted to leave.

"And so we say farewell to Ghastly Acres," he said,
and he flipped the keys into the air. Catching them behind his back, he turned and trotted down the creaky
porch steps. The boys followed him.

"Are you going to try to follow up that clue that the
ghost gave me?" asked Johnny eagerly. "I mean the one
about Crazy Annie, who has the key. You know what
I'm talking about, don't you?"

"Yes, John, I know what you are talking about," said
the professor primly. "But you must remember that
ghosts say lots of odd things that ordinary humans can't
possibly understand. Who is Crazy Annie, anyway? And
what kind of key is the ghost talking about? Is it a door
key, a skate key, the key of G, Francis Scott Key, or
what? You could spend hours or even years trying to
figure out the "Crazy Annie" clue, and in the end you
would probably come up with nothing. When I was
young I tried to solve impossible riddles, but I won't
try that kind of foolishness now!"

Again, Fergie and Johnny looked at each other. They were convinced that the professor was lying to them. When he got home, he was probably going to turn the world upside down to find out who Crazy Annie was and what her key was supposed to be. Well, if he thought he was going to leave Johnny and Fergie behind while he searched for clues, he had another think coming.

When they got back to Duston Heights that evening, the professor dropped Fergie off at his house and then drove to Fillmore Street, where he and Johnny's grandparents lived. The two old people were very surprised when Johnny walked in the front door lugging his suitcase, but they were happy to see him. The professor walked in after Johnny, and he told Gramma and Grampa Dixon a little story that he had made up on the way home. He said that the fishing had been bad and that life up in the wilds of Maine had been pretty dull, so they had decided to come home. As for the inheritance, he said that he would probably get it anyway because Perry's will was nutty and could be broken in court. After Johnny had had supper and talked with Gramma and Grampa for a while, he went across the street and helped the professor make a Sacher Torte, which is a very fancy Austrian chocolate layer cake. They played chess till they were both very sleepy and ready for bed. As he climbed the stairs to his bedroom that night, Johnny was thankful that no fearsome dark shapes would be hovering by his bedside or dragging him out on nightmarish journeys. But he kept thinking about the weird chessmen and the evil ruddy-faced man and Perry's insane poem, and he had a hunch that the strange sights and sounds they had seen at the old mansion were only a foretaste of worse things to come.

For a time the New England newspapers were full of the strange case of the disappearing comets. Astronomers were interviewed on radio and television, and they gave various explanations for the incredible extinguishing of the comets. Some said that the comets had been put out by the solar wind, or that they had been dying comets that just happened to go out at the same time. As usual there were people who claimed that the vanishing comets were a sign that the end of the world was near. But nobody paid much attention to them. Meanwhile August ended, and September arrived. Johnny and Fergie went back to school, and the professor started teaching history again at Haggstrum College. As the days passed, Johnny saw less and less of the professor. The old man had gotten secretive and sullen, and he kept to himself a lot. Now and then Johnny would glance out his bedroom window late at night and see Dr. Coote's old blue Chevrolet parked in front of the professor's house. Dr. Charles Coote taught at the University of New Hampshire, and he was an expert on magic and the occult. Whenever the professor consulted him, Johnny knew that something was up. But what, exactly, was up? Johnny would have given a lot to know.

One Saturday morning, to his very great surprise,

Johnny looked out the parlor window and saw a black Packard coupe pulling into the professor's driveway. When the car door opened, out stepped Dr. Highgaz Melkonian. Dr. Melkonian was a psychiatrist who had an office in Cambridge, and Johnny had been taken to see him once when the professor thought he needed help. The doctor was a short, burly man with a silky black beard and rippling black greasy hair. As usual he was dressed like someone who is getting ready to go to a wedding: gray cutaway, striped pants, and a pearl-gray ascot with a stickpin. As Johnny watched Dr. Melkonian amble toward the professor's front porch, he wondered what on earth the man was doing here. Had the professor suffered a mental breakdown? Was he losing his mind? Johnny became alarmed, and he began to imagine all sorts of frightful things, like the professor being strapped into a straitjacket and hustled away into a padded van by white-coated attendants. Then it occurred to him that Dr. Melkonian probably wouldn't have arrived if the professor had not called him up. So maybe things weren't that bad after all.

That afternoon Johnny decided to make up a reason for visiting the professor. He would tell him that he had left his ring binder with his algebra notes in the professor's house. With this in mind Johnny trotted across the street and climbed the front steps of the huge gray stucco house. But just as he was about to push the doorbell button, the professor stepped out.

"Good heavens, John Michael!" he exclaimed in a voice that was a little too loud and hearty. "Fancy meeting you here! Did you come over for cake or chess or just to talk?"

Johnny stared hard at the old man. He knew when the professor was covering something up. He always acted too jolly and wouldn't look you straight in the eye. "I just wanted to see if my ring binder was here," said Johnny. "Have you seen it anywhere?"

The professor coughed and looked away distractedly. "No . . . no, I can't say that I have. Hmph. You should be more careful about where you leave things. And now, if you don't mind, I have to get down to the post office before it closes."

As the professor brushed past him, Johnny smiled. He knew that the post office closed at noon on Saturday, and it was about half past three now. "Hey, Professor!" Johnny called. "Was that Dr. Melkonian who was here this morning? I thought it looked like his car."

The professor whirled suddenly. "Why—why, yes, it was," said the professor, staring at Johnny's shoes. "If you must know, he was . . . well, he was hypnotizing me."

Johnny's mouth dropped open. He had expected an excuse of some kind, but not this one. "How—how come you wanted to do that?" asked Johnny faintly.

By now the professor had recovered himself. He glared

at Johnny. "Because, my dear friend," he said, "I am an old man who keeps forgetting the historical facts that he used to know. It's embarrassing when I don't know when the Treaty of Westphalia was signed, or who was czar of Bulgaria in 972 A.D. So I thought I'd try to recover some of this information by having Dr. Melkonian hypnotize me. Now, if you don't have any more questions, I must be off. See you later."

With that the professor turned on his heel and stalked across the grass toward his car. Johnny watched him go, with a lot of confused thoughts rolling around in his mind. Slowly he started down the steps and then trotted along the sidewalk. He stood by the curb and waved at the professor as he drove off. Then, when the old man's car was out of sight, he spun around and headed back up the walk toward the front porch. Digging his hand into his pants pocket, Johnny pulled out the door key the professor had given him. Quickly he twisted the key in the lock and stepped into the front hall of the old house. He ran up the stairs to the professor's disorderly study. Heaps of term papers were piled on the floor, and the professor's desk was littered with cigarette ashes, paper clips, rubber bands, and pens. Flipping on the desk lamp, Johnny peered around, trying to see if the professor had left any clues as to what was going on in his mind these days. A cheap notepad lay on the desk blotter, and on it the professor had doodled flowers and butterflies and odd designs. He had also written several things:

Find out who Crazy Annie is.
Check burial records.
Astrology. When will he try again?

As Johnny read these things, he began to feel a bit smug—he had been right about the professor all along. He hadn't given up the fight against the evil Mr. Stallybrass. He had just pretended to give in, so that the boys would not be hurt. Well, said Johnny to himself, we're coming along whether he likes it or not! Snapping off the light, he marched downstairs and out the front door, locking it behind him. Then he went across the street to call up Fergie.

Johnny and Fergie went down to Peter's Sweet Shop, their favorite ice-cream store, and their special place for plotting and planning. As they sat in a booth and slurped malteds, they figured out what they were going to do. They would keep a very close watch on the professor. As soon as Johnny saw that Dr. Coote's car was at the old man's house, he would call up Fergie, and the two of them would sneak into the professor's house through a cellar window. They would take the back stairs up to the third floor and hide in one of the unused rooms above the professor's study so they could listen in on the conversation of the two old men through the hot-air register. Johnny had found out some time ago that hot-air vents in old houses made a perfect listening tube. As long as the vents were open—and they would be, on a chilly September night—the two boys would be able to eavesdrop. After that . . . well, after that they didn't know what was going to happen. For all they knew, the nasty Mr. Stallybrass was doing his dirty work up at the estate right now. Each night, before he went to bed, Johnny looked up at the sky. If everything seemed normal, he always heaved a sigh of relief. But he felt in his heart that they were living on borrowed time. How long did they have?

CHAPTER TEN

A few days later, as he was walking home from school, Johnny glanced across Fillmore Street and saw Dr. Coote's car parked in the professor's driveway. Immediately his heart began to beat faster, and his face flushed. Trying hard to stay calm, he walked quickly up the steps of his house and across the porch. When he opened the front door, he saw that Gramma was on the phone. Johnny's heart sank. He knew without asking that Gramma was talking to her cousin Elda, and when the two of them got on the phone, it sometimes took an hour to get them off. Biting his lip impatiently, Johnny walked into the living room and sat down in the bristly brown easy chair. He opened his history book and began to read, but he might as well have been trying to read a piece of wallpaper. He kept listening to the conversation that droned on in the hall, and he wondered when on earth Gramma would get off the line. Finally he heard the receiver click back into the cradle, and the chair by the phone creaked as Gramma got up and walked slowly back to the kitchen. When he was sure she had gone, Johnny got up and tiptoed into the hall.

The phone in Fergie's house rang fifteen times before someone finally picked it up. Luckily it was Fergie himself.

"Hi ho, big John! So what's up? Is—"

"He's here!" Johnny whispered hoarsely, "so you better get yourself in gear! Are you sure that cellar window is still loose?"

"Don't worry, it is. The prof never checks things like that."

Johnny scowled. He did not like spying on the professor, though in this case he felt he was doing it for a good cause. "Okay, just get on over here," he said, and then he hung up.

Around seven o'clock that evening, Johnny and Fergie were crouching on the cold, damp ground next to the foundation of the professor's house.

"Is this the window to the coal bin?" Johnny asked as Fergie edged forward and started prying at the glass.

Fergie snickered. "No, it ain't, John baby," he whispered in a mocking tone. "It's the window to the laundry room. If you're lucky, you'll catch your foot in a tub and break your ankle. But you won't get coal dust on your nice clean pants."

"Thanks," muttered Johnny sourly. He watched as Fergie gripped the window frame and shoved it inward. One at a time they slid over the sill on their stomachs. With a *thunk* Johnny's feet hit the bottom of a laundry tub. Awkwardly he hopped onto the floor, and Fergie came slithering into the room after him.

"There, now!" said Fergie, as he jumped down to join Johnny. "That wasn't such a big deal, was it? Where are those stairs?"

Johnny thought a bit. Then he pointed off to the left. "Over that way, I think. Come on."

By the thin, faint beam of Fergie's penlight the two boys made their way past dusty shelves to the foot of the back staircase. In days gone by the old house had had a staff of servants, and they had used this back stair as a way of getting around the house without disturbing the owners. The boys climbed, and the steps creaked loudly; Johnny imagined that the professor and Dr. Coote were hearing every little squeak and groan of the ancient wood. After what seemed like forever they opened a door to the third floor of the house, which was like a large attic with sloping ceilings. In one of the small rooms, once used as servants' quarters, an old dusty bed without any mattress stood in one corner, and there was a tiny brick fireplace with a boarded-up hearth. Set in the baseboard of one wall was a hot-air vent with an ornamental iron grill. The vent had been pulled shut. Johnny knelt to shove it open. As luck would have it, this room was directly over the professor's study. Almost instantly the boys began to hear the voices of the two old men, which sounded hollow and distorted. Apparently Dr. Coote was trying to explain something, but the professor kept butting in because he was not satisfied with the explanation.

"Now, wait a minute—just wait a minute!" growled the professor irritably. "Do you mean to say that this creep with the chessmen has taken over some kind of hocus-pocus that my brother began?"

Dr. Coote sighed. "Yes, Roderick. That is exactly what I mean. You have that diary that you found disguised as a cookbook in your brother's library. You have these letters that an Englishman named Edmund Stallybrass sent to your brother. It's pretty clear now that Perry was trying to frighten mankind into peacefulness by making comets zoom past the earth. It's a pretty crackbrained scheme, but your brother was not a terribly sane person, was he? All right, then. Your brother dies, and then this Englishman who stole the chessmen comes to America to put Perry's mad plan to work. However, I will bet you that our friend Stallybrass isn't interested in scaring mankind into peace. I think he has something a good deal more sinister in mind. It really is too bad that your brother chose to let this lunatic in on his plans, but I guess he needed him to steal the chessmen. I did a little digging and I found out that this Stallybrass used to be an assistant curator at the British Museum. It would have been easy for him to sneak into the museum at night."

The professor coughed and paused. "But see here, Charley," he said at last. "How did those two figure out that they could use a set of medieval chessmen as part of a magic ritual? It's not the sort of thing you read in museum guidebooks."

Dr. Coote sniffed. "No, Roderick, it most certainly is not! It beats me how they figured out their ritual, but . . . well, the British Museum has lots of old scrolls and books tucked away—things that no one has ever read. Maybe Stallybrass stumbled across something like that and then he wrote to Perry, and then the fun began!"

"Fun indeed!" growled the professor. "My brother should have been horsewhipped for even *thinking* of such a scheme! Well, now we have a crisis on our hands, but what can we do?"

"Roderick," Dr. Coote said slowly, "it seems clear that when you and the boys saw the comets vanish you must have seen a failed attempt. Or maybe it was just a trial run. But the question is, when will Stallybrass try again? I have combed through your dear brother's diary till my eyes ache, and I think I've finally figured out what all those astrological drawings were for."

"*Astrology!*" snorted the professor, "Leave it to my crackpot brother to believe in such rubbish! I told him many times—"

"You're forgetting something, my friend," said Dr. Coote, interrupting. "I will admit that the daily horoscopes in the papers are idiotic, but astrology was part of medieval magic. If we are going to stop Mr. Stallybrass, we have to take astrology seriously. Now, then— as far as I can figure out, Perry's magic ritual can only be used in a month when there is an eclipse of the moon, and when Jupiter and Saturn hang in conjunction in the house of Mars. I know that sounds like gobbledygook to you, but those conditions existed in August when our friend did his little magic routine. The planets won't be favorable again till mid-January, so we have a little time to plan a counterattack!"

Professor Childermass swore under his breath. "So we have time, do we?" he grumbled. "Time for what? Time to find out who Crazy Annie is? Do you know I have racked my brains, and I have even let myself be hypnotized, in order to find out who that woman is? But it's no good. Why on earth couldn't my brother's ghost have been a little clearer about what he meant?"

"Come now, Roderick," said Dr. Coote mildly. "You know as well as I do that ghosts have to speak in riddles—it has been this way ever since the dawn of time. The rules are ancient and must be observed."

"*Hmph!*" said the professor. "It seems to me that it is time the rules were changed! However, our problem remains: We have to go up to that wretched estate in the middle of the winter, and we have to fight without any weapons. What do you think our chances of winning are?"

"Pretty slim," retorted Dr. Coote with a weary sigh.

"But at least we have a little time to think. We need to go over this Crazy Annie business from every possible angle. You know, Crazy Annie could be a thing and not a person. Mons Meg was a cannon, and Jack-in-the-Pulpit is a flower. Do you see what I mean?"

"Yes, I do," the professor answered fiercely. "But I have combed the dictionaries and encyclopedias, and I can't find any plant or mineral or object whatever that is called Crazy Annie!" He sighed and blew his nose. "I'm not trying to be nasty, Charley," he went on in a milder tone, "but I'm afraid we're up against a big fat brick wall. Still, I'm not going to let Stallybrass have his way—not without a fight. I'm going to Perry's estate on January fifteenth. Will you come with me?"

Dr. Coote paused. "I'd love to, Roderick," he began nervously, "but as you know, I have bad legs and—"

"Oh, to the devil with your bad legs!" snapped the professor impatiently. "Bring a cane, for heaven's sake! I'm not asking you to be an Olympic runner, I'm just asking for moral support."

There was a longer pause. "Of course," said Dr. Coote. "Though I can't imagine what either one of us can do."

"Neither can I," said the professor gloomily. "It'll just be the old college try, the goal-line stand with two seconds remaining in the game." He added, in a voice that was thick with emotion, "Thanks for being my friend, Charley."

CHAPTER ELEVEN

The months rolled by, and the seasons changed. The maple leaves turned red and yellow and fell to the ground, and the cold winds of November whistled through the bare branches. In the first week of December snow fell on Fillmore Street, whitening the branches and piling little pointed caps on posts and fire hydrants. Mid-January was near, a lot nearer than Johnny and Fergie liked to think. Many times they had talked over the things they had heard while eavesdropping in the professor's attic. But now, as the fateful time got closer and closer, they realized that they didn't have a ghost of a plan. They wanted very much to help the two old men, but they didn't know how. Of course, the professor and Dr. Coote didn't have a plan either—all their hopes were pinned on finding out who Crazy Annie was. But what if they couldn't solve that riddle? Then the evil Mr. Stallybrass would be free to do whatever he liked, which was not a pleasant thing to think about. The boys felt hopeless, but they also felt determined. They wanted to be in on the adventure, even though it seemed like a very dangerous one.

They hashed over dozens of plans. They thought about stowing away in the trunk of the professor's car, but they realized that they would probably get locked in and have to bang for help in order to get out. If they hid in the backseat, one sneeze would betray them. So, one idea after another got shot down. But on a gray December afternoon, as the boys were gobbling hot fudge sundaes in their favorite booth at Peter's Sweet Shop, Fergie came up with the best scheme so far—they would take the train to Stone Arabia.

Johnny was startled by the idea. He held his dripping spoon in the air and stared in amazement at Fergie. "Do you think the train stops there?" he asked. "I mean, it's a really small town, and—"

"Be not worried, big John!" said Fergie with a confident grin. "I got a Boston and Maine timetable, and the choo-choo does stop there. We can hop the train the night those two old geezers drive up, an' then we can take a taxi out to the estate. They'll have to put us up for the—"

"Wait a minute!" said Johnny suddenly. "Where are we gonna get the money for all this?"

Fergie licked his spoon and looked smug. "From you, big boy. Remember when the prof gave you some money to start your own bank account? Well, if you haven't spent it all on chewing gum and Cracker Jacks, there oughta be enough left for a couple of train tickets and a taxi ride."

Johnny nodded weakly. But then another problem occurred to him. "What about our folks? We can't just say that we're taking off for Maine. What'll we tell them?"

Fergie grinned slyly. "I've got that one figured out too. You tell your gramma and grampa that you're stayin' over at my house for the night, an' I'll tell my folks that I'm stayin' at *your* house. They'll never check up on us, an' the next day we'll hitch a ride back with the prof and old Whosis. Nobody'll ever be the wiser."

Johnny paused and stared thoughtfully at the melting ice cream in his dish. "You don't think anything's really gonna happen when we go up there to the estate, do you?"

Fergie shook his head. He seemed calm and confident. "Naah, I really don't! That red-faced crumb blew it once when he tried all that abracadabra with the skull an' stuff. He might try again, but I think the prof and Dr. Coote will fix his clock. An' we're gonna help!"

Johnny looked at his friend doubtfully. Was Fergie just being brave, or did he honestly think that they could go up to Maine and face an evil magician without being harmed? The professor and Dr. Coote thought there was danger, and so did Johnny. And Johnny was not thrilled by Fergie's great big plan for fooling the Dixons and the Fergusons. Something could very easily go wrong. Gramma might call Mrs. Ferguson for a recipe, and then the beans would get spilled. But Johnny would not let his friend down. When Fergie climbed on the train, he would be with him, no matter what.

Christmas came, and Johnny got the usual presents from his grandparents—two white shirts, a tie, socks, and an outdoors novel called *North Woods Whammy*. The Dixons meant well, but they weren't very imaginative about gift giving. Then January arrived, with freezing gales and ice storms. The temperature dropped to near zero and stayed there for a week, and then it warmed up a bit and snowed. Now that the day for the professor's departure was getting closer, Johnny watched him like a hawk, listening for any hint of exactly when the trip would take place. He had said he'd go on the fifteenth, but he might get impatient and leave a day early. Finally, on the evening of the thirteenth, the professor casually told Johnny that he was going up to Durham the night of January fourteenth to visit Dr. Coote for a couple of days. As soon as he could, Johnny called Fergie and told him that the big trip was coming. The next morning, during breakfast, Johnny asked Gramma and Grampa Dixon if he could spend the night at Fergie's house. The next day was Saturday, and there would be no school, so Gramma and Grampa agreed.

Johnny spent his day at school in a very nervous state, with his stomach all knotted up and worried thoughts flitting through his brain. After school let out, he went down to the bank, drew out some money, and bought two railway tickets to Stone Arabia. Then he went home to pack his overnight bag.

Snow was falling steadily as Johnny stood on the yellow brick platform outside the Duston Heights railway station. He was wearing his old blue parka and red stocking cap, and he held a small black leather valise. He looked around nervously—where was Fergie? It was hard to believe that he would chicken out, but you never could tell. For the tenth time Johnny walked back into the heated station and peered up at the big electrical clock over the door. It said five minutes to seven. The train was due to be in the station at seven, and it would leave for Maine at ten after. "Fergie, you're cutting things pretty close," Johnny muttered under his breath. He bit his lip and looked around at the empty wooden benches and the potbellied iron stove. Maybe it would be a good thing if they did miss the train. Maybe the nervous voice that he heard in his head was his guardian angel telling him that this whole trip was a very bad idea, and that he'd better get out while he still had a chance. But just as Johnny was thinking that he should duck out the back door of the station and go home, Fergie walked in. He was wearing a tight-fitting leather jacket with a ratty fur collar and a pair of bright red fuzzy earmuffs and he had a bowling-ball bag that was obviously stuffed full of clothes. Fergie's cheeks were very red, and he was breathing hard.

"Sorry . . . to keep you waiting . . . John baby," he gasped as he sank down onto a bench. "My mom had a lot of chores for me to do, an' I thought I'd *never* get outa the house! Is the train in yet?"

As if in answer a long mournful wail sounded in the distance. Soon the big steel locomotive came thundering into the station, shooting off jets of steam. Johnny smiled weakly at his friend—he didn't know whether to be happy or sad. "Glad you made it," he said, not very sincerely. Together they headed out the door to the riveted steel steps that had just been lowered from one of the cars.

Johnny and Fergie sat in a smelly, dimly lit car and munched some candy bars they had brought with them. The only other passenger in the car was an elderly Catholic priest who was reading a small black book. Johnny put his head back on the wicker-covered seat and wished that he were asleep at home. This is all very crazy, he said silently. What are we gonna do once we get up there? How can we help the professor and Dr. Coote? Why did I ever agree to . . .

Johnny's head slipped to one side and he went to sleep. He was in the middle of a dream about a giant candy bar named Crazy Annie when he felt a hand shaking his shoulder.

"Huh? Wha—what is it?" mumbled Johnny thickly. He opened his eyes and found that a conductor in a navy-blue uniform was bending over him.

"Stone Arabia, young man," said the conductor in a

bored monotone. "Don't want to miss your stop. Lucky you fellas told me where you was gettin' off."

As Johnny removed his glasses and rubbed his eyes, the conductor reached over and shook Fergie, who was also asleep. Mumbling under his breath, Fergie came to life.

"Thanks, pal," he said, grinning stupidly at the conductor. Then he glanced across at Johnny, and he laughed. Johnny's stocking cap was stuck on the back of his head, and his hair was a mess. His glasses were crooked on his nose, and he looked crabby.

"Got your beauty sleep, didja?" asked Fergie with a chuckle.

Johnny gave him a dirty look. "Ho-ho," he muttered sarcastically. "You don't look all that great yourself!" He heaved a sigh and glanced out the window. The train was slowing down. "We're here," said Johnny in a voice that trembled. "I hope we can find a cab."

The train stopped, and the conductor bellowed, "Stone Arabia!" Wearily the boys stumbled to their feet and walked to the ridged steel platform outside the door of the car. Gripping the handrail, Johnny made his way down the steep steps to the ground, and Fergie came leaping down after him. Not far away was a little old-fashioned train station with a scallop-edged wooden roof and a fancy cupola. A weathered wooden sign said STONE ARABIA.

In the parking lot a taxi sat with its motor idling. Johnny grinned. He could hardly believe his eyes. It was at least eleven o'clock, and here was a cab waiting for them!

"Hey, John baby, we swing!" chortled Fergie as he stumbled forward through the snow. "I'll bet we get out to the mansion before the prof and his friend do!"

Johnny smiled wanly. He still had the front-door key that the professor had given him at the start of the summer visit, so they would be able to let themselves in. Nevertheless he was not happy about arriving at a cold, dark cavernous house in the middle of the winter. Gripping the handle of his valise tightly, he followed Fergie out to the waiting taxi. As they got closer to the cab, Johnny felt panicky, and he kept getting a strong urge to turn and run madly back to the train, which still stood in the station, blowing off clouds of steam. But Johnny told himself that he was being jittery over nothing, and he forced himself to plod forward through the white sparkling snow. As he stepped over a guard rail, he noticed that there was someone sitting in the backseat of the cab. At first this seemed strange, but then he thought, Oh, well, we're just going to be sharing a taxi ride with someone. As he reached forward to grasp the handle of the rear door, it was suddenly flung open.

Inside sat a hunched, shadowy figure, his face lit by a halo of trembling green light. It was the nasty red-faced man with the waxed mustache, and he held a small black leather case on his lap.

"Hello, boys," he said, sneering. "So nice to see you again!"

CHAPTER TWELVE

Before Johnny and Fergie could yell or run away, Mr. Stallybrass raised his left hand, and they were rooted to the spot. Their tongues stuck to the roofs of their mouths, and they could not speak. Moving woodenly, like two robots, the boys climbed into the back of the taxi. Mr. Stallybrass forced them to kneel on the floor and put their heads down on the seat. Then, with a triumphant smile, he told the driver where to go. For about ten minutes the taxi bumped and skidded along snowy roads until at last it turned into a lonely churchyard that was surrounded by a low stone wall. Snow blanketed the graves and rimmed the tops of the headstones, and at the top of a low rise a brick church could be seen. The cab crawled up the narrow drive till it stopped by the side of the dark, gloomy building.

"Ah, here we are at last!" said Mr. Stallybrass. He reached down and tapped each boy on the back. "Come on, lads! Let's go!"

The driver, an unshaven old man in a tattered overcoat, got out and opened one of the rear doors of the car. Mr. Stallybrass snapped his fingers, and the two boys clambered awkwardly onto the snowy drive and stood waiting with empty, staring eyes and half-open mouths. Taking his time, Mr. Stallybrass followed them. He reached into his pocket, took out a large brass key, and led the way to a low pointed door on the side of the church. It was bitterly cold now, and the snow had stopped. Sticking the key into the door, Mr. Stallybrass twisted it. The door opened with a scraping shudder, and as Johnny and Fergie were hustled forward by the two men, they saw worn stone steps leading down into the darkness. The boys clumped down the steps and through a low archway, guided by the pale beam of Mr. Stallybrass's flashlight. For a few minutes they halted while the driver searched for an oil lamp that he found at last in a cobwebbed corner. He managed to light the lamp, and a pale yellowish glow spread through the low-ceilinged chamber. The boys saw that they were in a burial vault under the church. Coffins lay in niches along the walls, and more were scattered on the rough earthen floor. Some of the coffin lids had brass plates that glimmered faintly in the light, while others had been smashed, so that you could see the bones inside. Two lidless coffins lay in the middle of the room, not far from the lamp. And in them Dr. Coote and Professor Childermass were laid out. Both were deathly pale and still, with folded hands and closed eyes. Were they dead?

A choked sob rose inside Johnny, and despair filled his heart. This was it, this was the end of his life and theirs. They had taken on an enemy who was too strong, and they had paid for it. Out of the corner of his eye Johnny saw Mr. Stallybrass step menacingly forward. He stopped near the two coffins and stood tapping the large key against his chin.

"So, there they are, lads!" he said calmly. "You see the result of rash actions and ill-thought-out plans! In case you were wondering, they're not dead . . . yet. However, they will be, when the temperature in this vault gets down to minus ten, as it should before morning. I've forced them to drink a strong sleeping potion, and that, together with the cold, ought to take care of them. As for you two, I'm going to have my grubby friend here tie you up and leave you with your dear old pals. I could immobilize you by magic, but that takes energy, and I have to save mine for later tonight. Besides, I want you two to squirm and struggle and know that there's no way of getting free. Very soon the planets will be in the right position for what I'm planning to do, and then . . . well, after that, the earth will be living on borrowed time. I'd explain what I mean, but surprises are best, aren't they? It's a pity that you two won't be around for the final act of my exciting little drama, but maybe that's just as well. By morning you charming lads will be as stiff and cold as those two elderly adventurers." Mr. Stallybrass paused, and his face slowly changed to a mask of cold, insane hatred. Flecks of white foam appeared at the corners of his mouth. "This is what must always happen to those who oppose me!" he snarled. "The heavens have decreed it!"

After a wild glance around the room Mr. Stallybrass motioned to the taxi driver, who stepped forward with a coil of rope and a knife in his hands. Johnny and Fergie were not paralyzed any longer, but they were frightened, so they did not resist as the driver tied their hands and feet and forced them to lie down on the ground. When the driver had done his work, Mr. Stallybrass snapped his fingers imperiously and motioned for the man to leave. But instead of leaving, he planted himself stubbornly in the middle of the floor and glared at his employer.

"Now, look here!" the man growled. "I've done everything you wanted, and more besides! You gave me some dough, but I want the rest, and I want *out*! I ain't doin' nothin' else till I get what's comin' to me!"

Mr. Stallybrass stared in silence at the man for a while, and then a sneer of contempt curled his lips. "Don't you tell *me* what to do, you miserable cur!" he said haughtily. "You will have more money, all that I promised, once you have helped me back at the mansion."

The man glowered sullenly at Mr. Stallybrass. "I just want what's mine," he grumbled. "That's all."

Mr. Stallybrass sighed. Then he chuckled unpleasantly and unbuttoned his overcoat. He pulled out four twenty-dollar gold pieces from his money belt and, with a flick of his wrist, he threw them to the driver, who thrust them into a pocket of his coat.

"There!" snapped Mr. Stallybrass. "Are you satisfied for now? Good! Then let us leave these not-so-charming people and go to our next task."

The driver nodded glumly and followed Mr. Stallybrass out of the vault. With fear in their hearts the boys heard the door slam and the key turn in the lock. For several minutes they lay still and listened to their hammering hearts. Clouds of cold breath poured from their mouths, and they glanced hopelessly around. Then they began to struggle. Wildly Johnny and Fergie thrashed around on the cold dirt floor. But even after they had exhausted themselves, they still were securely tied. With a mighty effort Fergie wrenched himself into a sitting position and looked around. The oil lamp still burned and the professor and Dr. Coote lay stiff and unmoving.

"This sure looks bad!" gasped Fergie, who was out of breath because he had struggled so much. "I—I hate to be gloomy, but maybe this is the end for all of us!"

Johnny closed his eyes. He could feel the numbing cold seeping into his bones. Soon he would have that awful feeling of sleepiness that comes when you are freezing to death. He had read of such things in Jack

London stories, but he never thought that he would face a death like that himself. Johnny racked his brain desperately. Wasn't there anything *anyone* could do? Fergie began to scuttle sideways. Grabbing a brass handle that hung from one side of a coffin, he lurched upward and came down on top of the coffin's lid. The rotten wood gave way, and Fergie sank down among bones and bits of rotten cloth.

"Oh, great!" he exclaimed. "Now what do I do?"

Johnny started to cry. Big tears trickled out of the corners of his eyes, and the bitter taste of salt filled his mouth. This was really it, this was the end. They would die miserably, all four of them. Weeping steadily, Johnny gave in to utter despair. He had never felt worse in his life, and he was utterly convinced that death was near. But as he sniffled and cried, he heard a slight sound as if some animal—a dog, maybe—was pawing at the door of the vault.

"Hey!" exclaimed Fergie. "It's a doggie! Shows there's life somewhere in this crummy burg!" Frantically Fergie tried to heave himself up out of the wreckage of the coffin, but with a loud, splintering crash he sank back down again. "Great!" he exclaimed angrily. "If I ever get my hands on that beefy-faced crud, I'm gonna—"

Fergie's voice died. The door of the vault shuddered open with a loud *crrrunk!* and a wavering patch of light fell across the floor. A short, odd-looking old woman with a flickering railroad lantern in her hand stepped through the doorway. Her clothing looked as if it had been rescued from a ragbag—the skirt was a patchwork quilt that fell to the floor, and her blouse was wrinkled and stained with berry juice. Her face was round and doughy, and she wore very thick glasses. A heap of untidy gray hair was held in place by a dirty polka-dotted ribbon.

The woman tottered into the vault. "Mercy!" she exclaimed as she sat down on a carved block of stone. "What are you people doing here? You'll die of the cold if you're not careful!"

CHAPTER THIRTEEN

"We didn't have much choice about bein' here, lady!" grumbled Fergie. "Some rotten egg tied us up an' left us here. Hey, have you got a knife on you?"

The woman smiled and fumbled at her broad leather belt. A small flat pouch hung there, and from it she drew a tiny bone-handled jackknife. Opening one of the blades, she stepped forward and began sawing at the ropes that tied Fergie's wrists. In a few seconds he was free. A little more sawing, and Johnny was free too.

"Boy, that feels great!" Fergie exclaimed as he heaved himself to his feet. "You came just in time, lady!" Then he paused. A thought had occurred to him. "What made you come here, anyway?"

The woman looked embarrassed. "Well, if you must know," she said shyly, "I'm a witch. And the recipes and potions I use call for ingredients like scrapings from skulls and ground coffin wood. I come here when I absolutely have to have something that I can't get anywhere else. I do hope you won't report me to the—"

"Please, lady!" exclaimed Johnny, cutting in suddenly. "We don't have time to talk! A couple of our friends are down there on the floor, and we have to help them! The guy that tied us up gave 'em some kind of sleeping potion, and if they aren't dead already, they will be if they stay where they are. Can you do something?"

For the first time the old woman noticed the two men lying side by side in their coffins. She went to Professor Childermass, knelt down, and pressed two fingers of her right hand to his forehead. Then in a singsong voice she said:

Life return, potions fade
Dwell no longer in the shade
Blood of bat, howlet's wing
Come awake, these slumbers fling!

At first nothing happened, but soon the color came flooding back into the professor's cheeks. He coughed and blinked, and then with a jerk he sat up.

"My gosh, she really *is* a witch!" gasped Fergie.

After giving Fergie a dirty look the old woman moved

over to Dr. Coote and began using the spell on him. Meanwhile the professor glanced with astonishment at the boys, adjusted his glasses and began studying the old woman. Suddenly a light came on in his brain. He was guessing wildly, but he was convinced that his guess was right.

"*Crazy Annie!*" he exclaimed. "*You're* the one we're supposed to be looking for!"

The woman turned and wrinkled up her nose disdainfully. "I'll thank you not to use that nickname," she said coldly. "Mean children and your worthless brother have called me that, but I find the name offensive. My name is Anna Louisa Thripp—Mrs. Thripp to you!" She went back to the job of reviving Dr. Coote.

The professor climbed out of the coffin and stood there brushing dirt off his coat. A look of astonishment was on his face. "How the devil do you know that I'm Perry Childermass's brother?" he asked. "As far as I know, I've never met you in my life!"

"I guessed who you were," snapped Mrs. Thripp without looking up. "All you Childermasses are alike: short and cranky and opinionated, and you don't know how to comb your hair. Perry mentioned to me once or twice that he had some rather disagreeable brothers, but I never expected to meet them. By the way, what is all this nonsense about looking for me? Are you?"

"Yes!" said the professor excitedly. "My brother—or rather, his ghost—said that you could help us fight an evil wizard who is at the old mansion right now, trying to do something indescribably awful!"

Dr. Coote groaned and began to stir. Mrs. Thripp helped him sit up and then got to her feet. "Do you mean that Englishman with the mustache and the surly attitude? I passed him on the street one day, and I felt his power. So what is he trying to do?"

While Dr. Coote rubbed circulation back into his arms and legs, the professor explained about the comets, the chessmen, and the skulls. As he talked, Mrs. Thripp's stare grew hard, and the set of her mouth got grimmer.

"So *that's* his game!" she said indignantly. "I should have known he was up to no good!" Then her manner changed, and she looked sad. "But I can't imagine why your brother sent you to me," she went on gloomily. "I'm really not very powerful. If you want me to cure the sniffles or make someone fall in love, I can probably help. But it sounds as if this Englishman is a big-league heavy hitter, and I'm afraid I'm not. Sorry!"

The professor was getting exasperated. But he fought down his crabbiness and smiled as politely as possible. "But, madam!" he began, in a pleading tone. "My brother *must* be right! About your being able to help, I mean. His ghost spoke to John here and said that you had the key. Those were his words!"

Mrs. Thripp laughed heartily. "The key!" she exclaimed. "I'll say I have the key! I have bushels of keys." She added, in a sheepish voice, "If you want to know, I also save string."

"But you do have keys!" exclaimed the professor as he clutched at the woman's arm. "Are any of them magic?"

The woman gazed at him blankly. "Not that I know of."

The professor was getting more anxious. "See here, madam," he began, "we may not have a lot of time, but . . . well, could you take us to your house and show us these keys?"

Mrs. Thripp hesitated and then she smiled. "Well, if you think it will help, I'll—"

"Thanks a million!" snapped the professor, cutting her off. He turned to Dr. Coote and the two boys, who were staring at him with their mouths open. "Come on, everybody!" he said with a wave of his arm. "We're going over to Mrs. Thripp's house."

The professor grabbed Mrs. Thripp's lantern and led the way out of the gloomy, cold crypt into the churchyard. Even though the air was bitingly cold, Johnny and Fergie sucked it into their lungs—they had never been so glad to get out of a place in their lives. It was an odd little procession that wound its way past the snow-covered headstones, with the professor and his bobbing lantern in the lead. As it turned out, Mrs. Thripp's house was just across the road and down a little wooded lane. She lived in a squat, shabby bungalow with a gambrel roof and a screened porch. Nailed to a tree next to the house were red taillight reflectors and old license plates; a small straw doll hung from the handle of the screen door. As the visitors walked into the house, they noticed that it smelled strongly of beef stew and wood smoke. A dusky oil painting of a bird dog hung above the mantel of the fieldstone fireplace, and overstuffed chairs stood on the threadbare rug. The window shades were ragged and patched with old newspaper comic strips, and by the refrigerator a black cat was lapping milk from a cracked willowware saucer. Without a word Mrs. Thripp led her guests to the tiny kitchen, and there on a table stood a large cardboard carton that had once held boxes of laundry soap. In it were heaps and heaps of keys. Keys of all kinds and sizes and shapes, wired together or tied in bunches with twine, or just thrown loose into the box.

The professor's heart sank. How would he ever manage to figure out which of these keys was the right one? And then, after he found it—*if* he found it—he would have to go racing over to the mansion and—and do what? He didn't have the slightest idea. Not the faintest ghost of one. As he stared at the unholy mess of rusting keys, the professor felt real despair. How much time did they have? He didn't know that either. After scooping up a handful of keys he flung them down in disgust and gazed about distractedly. He really had to find out how late it was. When Mr. Stallybrass made his first attempt with the chessmen, the climax of the sorcery came at midnight. So they had to get over to the mansion before then. But the professor had left his watch in his car, so he had to consult a clock. Every kitchen had a clock, so where was Mrs. Thripp's?

Suddenly the professor stopped and stared. An iron bracket was bolted to the wall above the table, and from it hung three or four flower-print dresses on hangers. They were nothing special—strictly Salvation Army stuff—but a small piece of costume jewelry was pinned to the one that hung on the outside. It was covered with twinkling rhinestones and was shaped like a key.

The professor let out a bloodcurdling screech and pointed with a trembling finger at the key. *"That's it!"* he yelled. Whirling around, the professor grabbed Mrs. Thripp by the arm. "Tell me quick!" he barked. "Is that piece of jewelry magic? *Is it?"*

Mrs. Thripp looked startled, but then she smiled vaguely. "Well, no. Or maybe I should say yes, it is . . . in a way. I mean, it's one of the things I tried to enchant once upon a time, long ago." She paused and then went on slowly. "You see, when I was starting out as a witch I tried a lot of spells, just for practice. I enchanted flatirons and geraniums and all sorts of silly things. I don't recall what sort of spell I put on that pin, but whatever it was, it seems to have failed. I can assure you that the pin is about as magical as your grandma's nightie."

The professor bit his lip impatiently. Then suddenly he snapped his fingers. "We'll have to try it," he said grimly. "It's our only chance! Will you put on that pin and come with us to Perry's old mansion?"

Mrs. Thripp looked confused, but she nodded. "Yes, of course, if you think it will help," she said. "By the way," she went on, "you seemed to be looking around for a clock a few minutes ago. Mine's broken, but my old Benrus says that it's half past eleven."

"So we still have time!" exclaimed the professor. "Great! But how do we get to that dratted estate from here? Do you know the way?"

"Certainly," Mrs. Thripp answered. "I used to go there a lot and talk with Perry . . . usually about magic. I'd say the place is about four miles from here. We can use my car."

The professor, Johnny, Fergie, and Dr. Coote all cheered. This was better than any of them had expected. With a lot of fumbling Mrs. Thripp got the rhinestone pin off the blouse on the hanger and pinned it to the one she was wearing. Then she led her visitors out through a back door and down a narrow walkway to her very untidy garage, which smelled of paint and engine oil. There stood a rusty 1947 Nash, which looked a bit like an upside-down bathtub with windows. Reaching up onto a shelf, Mrs. Thripp brought down a key ring from which a small plastic skull hung. With a little bow she handed the keys to the professor.

"I don't actually drive myself," she said, "because I have poor eyesight. My brother lives near here, and he usually comes over to cart me around when I need to go someplace."

"Thank you, madam," said the professor brusquely. "Byron, will you see if you can open the garage doors, while I get this rust bucket started? The rest of you climb in and cross your fingers."

Mrs. Thripp looked offended when the professor called her car a rust bucket, but she got into the front seat next to him, while Johnny and Dr. Coote climbed into the back. Meanwhile Fergie struggled with the old-fashioned folding doors of the garage. At first the professor got nothing but a halfhearted whine from the car's ignition system. But he tried again and again, and finally the engine turned over. He nosed the rattly old car onto the snowy road, while Mrs. Thripp gave him directions. The two-lane blacktop was not very well plowed, and a layer of hard-packed snow lay under them. The car steered awkwardly, and it skidded and fishtailed as the professor rounded the curves. But no one complained about the old man's driving—they all knew this was an emergency.

As they drove on, the professor began to recognize the road he had been on many times during the summer. He saw a familiar catalpa tree that leaned out from an overhanging snowbank, and a wooden mailbox holder made in the shape of Uncle Sam. They crawled up the long hill that led to the gates of Perry's estate. As the car ground forward, it slowed down. The tires spun and whined, and the professor pressed down on the accelerator, but it was no good. They went slower and slower, till the car stopped and began to slide backward.

The terrified passengers clung to armrests and prayed as the car rolled back to the bottom of the hill and buried its rear end in a snowbank.

Silence fell. The professor turned off the engine and pounded angrily on the steering wheel with his fists. *"Blast it all anyway!"* he roared. Then a thought occurred to him. Turning to Mrs. Thripp, he smiled in a strained way. "Madam," he said coldly, "is it possible that you don't have snow chains on this car?"

"Snow chains?" said Mrs. Thripp in a wondering tone. "I—I don't think I have them. I mean, I don't go about much in the winter, and—"

"Great!" snapped the professor, cutting her off. "Just great! Fortunately we aren't terribly far from the estate. We are all going to have to get out and walk! Come on children, hop to it!"

Groaning, Dr. Coote and the boys climbed out of the car and began slogging up the snowy road. The professor marched along briskly, and so did Mrs. Thripp, who was really a better hiker than you might have expected. Johnny looked up as a comet flashed across the cold, starry sky. Frightened, Johnny struggled to catch up to the professor, who was near the top of the hill.

"Pro—Professor," gasped Johnny as he plodded alongside the old man, "is—is that thing up there—"

"I don't know what it is," snapped the professor, putting his head down and resolutely marching forward. "But if I were you I'd save my breath. You'll need it if you're going to get to the mansion without collapsing."

They struggled on. The shadowy gateposts of the estate could be seen now, and to everyone's great surprise the driveway to the mansion was plowed!

"He . . . must have done it . . . for his own convenience," gasped the professor, as he paused to catch his breath. "Well, without meaning to, the fool has made it easier for us! Come on!"

Johnny's legs felt like rubber, and he kept wanting to collapse, but he forced his feet to move. Finally he saw the mansion in the distance. Light blazed from every window, but the tower room was ominously dark. The house looked the way it had on that summer night when the comets died.

"Lovely, eh?" said Fergie, as he stomped alongside Johnny. "I wonder what the prof and Mrs. Whosis are gonna do if we can't get near the place."

"That would indeed be a problem, Byron," said the professor, who was walking nearby. "However, we should not give up hope until all hope is gone. It's ten minutes to midnight by Mrs. Thripp's watch—let's see how close we can get."

The path that led from the driveway to the front door of the mansion had been shoveled, so the five of them walked on it, with the professor in the lead. This time there was no invisible barrier, and they clumped up the porch steps to the entrance. When he opened the door, the professor gasped. A frozen waterfall had cascaded down the front stairs, and the hall looked like a skating rink.

"Good heavens!" exclaimed the professor. "A pipe must have burst somewhere! I should have had the water turned off when I left, but we don't have time to think about that now. Fortunately, there's a back staircase, and let us hope that the upstairs of the house doesn't look like the Scott Glacier! This way, and try not to fall down!"

Slipping and sliding, everyone followed the professor down the hall to the back of the house. Frost-rimmed paintings stared down on them as they passed, and clouds of breath hung in the air—it was bitterly cold, colder even than it was outside. When he got to the back stairs, the professor was glad to see that the steps were bare. Waving for the others to follow, he started up. Johnny felt so nervous that he was ready to jump out of his skin, and he kept glancing at Fergie. Fergie plodded along with his head down, his mouth set in a grim frown.

At the top of the stairs they came out onto the second floor. The hall lights were on, and the floor was dry except for a patch of ice that lay outside the door of the bathroom. Picking his way carefully, the professor moved to the narrow stair that led to the dark forbidding door of the tower room. In the distance they could hear a droning chant, a weird muttering sound that ran down the sloping ceiling of the stairwell. With Mrs. Thripp right behind him the professor started up. The blood was singing in his ears, but anger and crankiness drove him on. At last he stood before the paneled door. He raised his hand to knock, but quite unexpectedly the heavy door swung open. What he saw made the professor gasp and step back involuntarily.

CHAPTER FOURTEEN

The ugly boarded-up tower room was lit by a forest of candles. They burned in tall and short holders, in black crusty candelabra and china dishes, and their yellow smoky flames flickered in the draft from the open door. In the middle of the room was a low brass table, and the warped chessboard had been placed on it. The bug-eyed walrus ivory chessmen had been arranged on the chessboard—some in rows and some in a little circle. A blood-streaked human skull stared grimly down from the mantelpiece, and its empty eyes seemed to wink in the candlelight. Standing near the table was Mr. Stallybrass in a black velvet robe. A medallion shaped like a flaring sun hung from a golden chain around his neck. His face was even more flushed than usual, and rivulets of sweat were running down his cheeks. But he seemed triumphant and calm. In one hand he held a long wooden pointer with a silver star on the end. In the other he clutched a small book with a black leather cover.

"My oh my, it's a welcoming committee!" he said mockingly. "I'd invite you in, but I'm not feeling very hospitable at present. In fact, if you try to come in, you will be stopped."

"Oh, really?" said the professor as he took a step forward. Suddenly he felt something like an electrical shock and jumped hastily back.

Mr. Stallybrass laughed. "You see what I mean, don't you? Actually, I didn't need to let you come this far, but I wanted you all to witness this fascinating ceremony. It was dreamed up ages ago by unknown wizards. Dear old Perry found a rather incomplete version of the ritual, and he tried to use it. The results were not too good, however, and he began writing to me. Well, I rummaged in the basement of the British Museum and came up with a handwritten book of magic from the twelfth century. It has a more complete version of the rite, although one or two words are hard to read—but I'll return to that later." He walked forward and tapped the chessboard with his wand. "This new improved version," he went on, "includes the little chessmen you see here, and as you probably have guessed, I pinched them. At first I thought of working together with Perry on this grand plan, but it occurred to me that he would probably want to stick to his silly scheme of frightening people into peacefulness by using the comets." Mr. Stallybrass laughed harshly and walked over to the fireplace. He grinned evilly.

"I had a better plan!" he continued. "A *much* better one! If comets were to wipe out nearly all human life on earth, and if I were one of the few humans to survive, then I could rule those who were left. Perhaps, when this ceremony is completed, I will become a spirit with godlike powers. There are some hints of that in the magic book, though they're a bit vague. At any rate, I decided to come up here and poison poor Perry. Then I had to wait around for the planets to be in the proper conjunction. In the meantime you showed up, you silly little man. You and those loutish boys witnessed my first attempt, but I'm afraid it was not a success. I had misinterpreted some important words in the book. My Latin is not as good as it once was, and the monkish script is *very* hard to read. I had been using old skulls from long-dead people. Perry had done the same thing— we got them from that vault I locked you into. Well, it seems that we were wrong. Last fall I had the parchment X-rayed, and found out that I had been misreading some words. What you need, it seems, is the skull of a *freshly killed* human. Sooo . . . I found someone who wouldn't be missed, pretended to befriend him, and there he is up on the mantelpiece. It's the man who was driving the taxi—I'm sure the boys remember him."

"My Lord!" gasped the professor as he put his hand over his face. "How awful!"

Mr. Stallybrass laughed harshly. "Oh, spare me your humanitarian horror, please! You're just like your brother—afraid to do things that will help you achieve greatness."

"You call that greatness, murdering someone?" put in Mrs. Thripp who was standing right behind the professor. "Murder is wrong, regardless of who does it or what he thinks he'll achieve."

Mr. Stallybrass walked forward and peered curiously over the professor's shoulder. "Oh, it's *you*, is it?" he said nastily. "Aren't you the local witch, the one they call Crazy Annie? Did you come up here to try out your homemade magic on me? Well, all you get to do, dear lady, is watch. In a few minutes that burning comet will swerve toward earth, and that will be just the beginning. In a few months' time a rain of comets will hit the earth, causing unbelievable destruction. That's a little out of your league, isn't it, dearie?"

Mrs. Thripp opened her mouth to say something, but at that moment Stallybrass gestured with his wand, and a leaping blue flame shot from the left eyesocket of the skull to the chessboard. Instantly all the chessmen were lit with green haloes of light, and the floor of the room shook. The candles trembled in their sockets. Stallybrass turned to the skull, raised his arms, and began a long chant in Latin. Letters of fire appeared in the air over the table, Hebrew letters that were used in the rituals of the Kabbala. The professor watched in frozen horror. Behind him he could hear Dr. Coote and the boys praying—they were saying the Our Father loudly and fervently. But if the prayer had any magic in it, it was not working—the hellish rite went on.

Mrs. Thripp stood silent, with a strange look on her face. Then—quite suddenly—she elbowed the professor out of the way and stepped forward. With two fingers of her right hand pressed to the rhinestone pin, she moved into the room, past the invisible barrier. Immediately the blue flames and the green haloes died. The fiery letters disappeared, and the candle flames sputtered. With a look of fear and rage on his face Stallybrass turned to Mrs. Thripp. He laid down his book and wand and stepped forward to challenge her.

"You foolish old hag, how did you get in here?" he snarled. "No doubt you used some trick from your jim-dandy magic cookbook! Well, prepare to die! And when I have thrust your body into the outer darkness, I will go on with my work!"

Stallybrass raised his hand, but Mrs. Thripp calmly unpinned the key-shaped ornament and held it out for him to take. Mr. Stallybrass didn't want to touch it, but he had no choice. Unseen forces thrust his hand forward, closing his fingers around the small glittering object.

"*Pale Hecate, Queen of Witches, bids me give you this,*" said Mrs. Thripp, in a voice that echoed oddly. "*All thy spells are now o'erthrown!*"

Mr. Stallybrass tried to throw the pin away, but his

hand stayed clamped around it. He raged and staggered back and forth, but it was no good. Then, suddenly, with a loud splintering sound, the boards that covered one of the tall narrow windows broke apart, and a strong wind rushed into the room. The candles flickered and went out, but tongues of fire appeared near the ceiling. Seven flames there were, hovering motionless and feeding on the empty air. Stallybrass fell to his knees, sobbing. He muttered brokenly and tried to ask forgiveness, but it was all in vain. A roaring gale seized him and swept him out into the night, and an earsplitting wail sounded in the room. Mrs. Thripp and the others fell to their knees and covered their ears. The inhuman hooting sound went on and seemed to be inside the marrow of their bones, and then it was gone. The bare bulb overhead came on and the room was bathed in harsh, glaring light.

"Goodness!" exclaimed Mrs. Thripp as she dragged herself to her feet. "I had no *idea* that would happen!" Blinking vaguely she turned to the professor. "Excuse me, what did I say? I know it was something grand sounding, but I can't remember what it was."

With tears in his eyes the professor rushed forward and hugged the old woman. "I'll tell you some other time," he said in a voice that was thick with emotion. "But you said the right thing, that's for certain!"

"I'll say!" exclaimed Dr. Coote, who had suddenly come rushing into the room. Awkwardly he reached out and shook Mrs. Thripp's hand. "Jolly good show! Did you know that your pin would have that kind of effect on him?"

Mrs. Thripp shook her head vigorously. "Good heavens, no! When I stepped into the room I . . . well, I felt as if some force outside myself had taken over. I said things that I would never have dreamed of saying in a thousand years!"

"Well, however it happened, you did a wonderful job!" said the professor exultantly. "I will always remember the look on that rotten man's face when he . . ."

His voice trailed off as he noticed that Mrs. Thripp was not paying any attention to him. She was walking back and forth with her head down, and suddenly she let out a sharp exclamation and dropped to her knees. Happily she raised her hand, and in it was the key-shaped rhinestone pin.

"Thank goodness I found it!" she exclaimed as she stood up and fastened it to her blouse. "I was afraid that horrible man had taken it with him. It's not worth much, but . . . well, you never know when you may want a piece of costume jewelry. For special occasions, I mean."

CHAPTER FIFTEEN

At three in the morning the boys, Dr. Coote, and the professor were sitting in Mrs. Thripp's living room, sipping hot cider. They were all pretty tired, because they had to dig the Nash out of the snowbank. Fortunately there weren't any steep hills on the way back, so once they got the car started, the rest was fairly easy. Everything that had happened to them on this night seemed like a very strange dream, except they all knew it was true. "My, that's *good*!" said the professor as he sipped. Suddenly a thought occurred to him, and he looked up. "By the way," he said, "how did you manage to get into the church's vault to save us? Did you use magic to open the door?"

Mrs. Thripp looked surprised. "Heavens, no!" she said. "I used a key! I told you that I am nuts about keys, and so I stole the key to the vault from the nail where it hung in the chapel. I'm not terribly proud of the midnight raids I used to make into that gloomy place, but I was always very neat and respectful about what I did— unlike that beefy-faced oaf, who seems to have smashed some coffins open with an axe. When I saw that, I knew something was up, but I had no idea what. And I could hardly tell the police because I would have had to admit that I had been in the vault myself." She paused and sighed. "And to think that Perry just wanted to frighten humans into peace by means of those comets! It was a nice idea, but not a very practical one."

"No, it certainly was not," said Dr. Coote, who was sitting on the sofa and puffing at his briar pipe. "For one thing, how was he going to convince people that the comets were sent by an angry God to warn them against their warlike ways? Was he going to seize a television network and pretend to be an angel handing out the bad news?"

The professor chuckled and shook his head. "I honestly don't think Perry ever worked out the practical part of his plan. He was well meaning but scatter-brained. Unfortunately he ran into Stallybrass, who was logical, cold blooded, and efficient. He had a plan, all right—a plan for total destruction!"

Johnny shuddered and slurped at his cider. "Do you

know who stole Perry's body, Professor?" he asked timidly. "Was it Mr. Stallybrass? And did he do it because he wanted to use Perry's skull for—for—"

"For his devil magic?" put in Dr. Coote. "I would say, probably not. I will admit that I think you are right in guessing that Stallybrass broke open the tomb and stole the corpse. But he could get skulls from the church vault if he wanted them, and at that time he didn't realize he was misreading the magic ceremony. I think that wretched man stole the body in order to frighten the professor and you two boys away from the estate. After all, it would have been a lot easier for him if the mansion had stayed empty all summer. He wouldn't have had to sneak around in order to set things up in the tower room. Luckily you three didn't scare so easily. You came back and settled his hash, but good!"

Mrs. Thripp coughed. "With a little help, you might add," she said, making a small mock-polite bow. "You folks knew what the ghost had said, but you wouldn't have gotten very far without my lovely rhinestone pin."

"No, we certainly wouldn't have," said the professor thoughtfully. He set his cider mug down on the coffee table and looked up at Mrs. Thripp. "Do you suppose I could see your pin for a minute?" he asked suddenly.

Mrs. Thripp looked surprised, but then she smiled, unfastened the pin, and handed it to the professor. Thoughtfully he turned the object over in his hands.

The back was smooth and plated with silver, and words were engraved there:

Thou shalt break them with a rod of iron; thou shalt dash them in pieces like a potter's vessel.

"Heavens!" he said in astonishment. "Did you have these words put here, Mrs. Thripp?"

The old woman bent over and peered at the pin. Then she shook her head in wonderment. "No," she said with a strange smile. "There was nothing there at all when I bought the pin, or after I enchanted it. Those words must have appeared tonight, when we . . ." Her voice trailed off and she sat down, rubbing her chin.

For a long time everyone just sipped cider quietly and said nothing. Fergie had been strangely silent all night, but when he had finished the last of his cider, he spoke. There was a mischievous gleam in his eye.

"Hey, Prof," he said slyly, "what are you gonna do with those chessmen? They must be worth a lot of dough and you know what they say—finders keepers!"

The professor coughed grumpily. "Byron," he said acidly, "you are suggesting a dishonest course of action. Those chessmen belong in the British Museum, and they are going back there as soon as I can figure out how to return them. Unfortunately I can't just go to the local police and say "Here they are," because then everyone would think that I stole them. I will probably put them in a box, wrap the box in brown paper and twine, and airmail it to Scotland Yard in London. The chief inspector can have the pleasure of returning the little fellows to the museum. And when we go back to the mansion tomorrow, I will destroy that priceless twelfth-century magic book and chop the chessboard into kindling wood. Without them no one will ever be able to reconstruct that vile, detestable ritual."

"Speaking of the estate," put in Dr. Coote, "what are you going to do about it? You violated the terms of Perry's will when you went home last August. Will you try to break the will?"

The professor looked thoughtful. "I suppose I could break the will if I tried," he said slowly, "but it would take a lot of time and lawyers' fees and I just don't think it would be worth it. I have enough money to last me for the rest of my lifetime. All my brothers are dead now, so I suppose the money and the mansion will go to one of their worthless children. I don't care—I wash my hands of the whole filthy business!" He turned to Dr. Coote and pointed a knobbly finger at him. "As for you, Charley," he said solemnly, "if you ever hear me talking about a get-rich-quick scheme again, I hope you kick me good and hard."

Dr. Coote smiled blandly. "It will be a pleasure, Roderick," he said. "Mrs. Thripp here will immobilize you with a magic spell while I apply the boot."

"Wait a minute!" exclaimed the professor nervously. "You shouldn't take everything I say so seriously! I mean, suppose I figure out a foolproof way of winning at poker? Then will you—"

"We'll kick you around the block," laughed Dr. Coote. "It'll be for your own good."

"Oh, thanks!" said the professor sourly. "Everyone is always thinking of me!"

CHAPTER SIXTEEN

The adventure was supposed to be over, but it wasn't. The boys went back to their normal lives in Duston Heights, and as the months passed they heard bits and pieces of news. The estate of Stone Arabia had been sold to a real estate developer, who wanted to build houses on the land. The professor had lost his chance at the ten million, but he had gotten twenty thousand dollars as a consolation prize. The body of Mr. Stallybrass had been found, horribly mutilated, in the Kennebec River. The body of Perry Childermass had not been found, and the police had given up the search. Then, one day in April, the professor announced to the boys that he was going to England to return the chessmen, and he was inviting them to go along. They would leave in June, as soon as school was out. The boys were delighted.

"I thought you were gonna send the chessmen back in a little box and not say who they were from," said Johnny.

Patiently the professor explained. He had consulted legal authorities, and they had assured him that he wouldn't be prosecuted if he brought them back. In fact, the British Museum was offering a reward of three thousand pounds for their safe return, and that would be more than enough to pay for a trip to London for the professor and the two boys.

So, one sunny day in June, the old man and his friends were standing before the pompous doorway of the British Museum. After snapping a picture of Fergie and Johnny in front of the fluted Greek columns of the entrance, the professor led the way in. They spent a couple of hours gawking at the treasures—Egyptian statues and Assyrian winged bulls, rows of Egyptian mummies and clocks and curios of all sorts. Finally they came to the room where the chessmen were kept under glass. Hesitantly Johnny and Fergie approached the display case. They were fearful without really knowing why. Johnny kept telling himself that the chessmen were perfectly harmless now, but a lot of nagging doubts remained in his mind. These odd little objects had been used in a ritual that nearly destroyed the world. Mr. Stallybrass was dead, but maybe another sorcerer would know how to use the chessmen.

The professor glanced sharply at Johnny, and he read his thoughts. "Worried, John?" he asked in a taunting voice. "Are you afraid that the little beggars will come crawling out of their glass case and do a tango in the middle of the floor?"

Johnny stared sullenly at the floor. "Aw, come on, Professor!" he grumbled. "Stop making fun of me! If you really want to know, yeah, I am worried, because maybe there might be another copy, somewhere, of that magic ritual that Mr. Stallybrass tried to use."

The professor shook his head firmly. "No, John," he said. "I do *not* think it is possible! That magic book that we burned was done by hand, before printing was invented. The chances of there being another one like it are . . . well, I would say a million to one against."

Johnny seemed a bit reassured, but Fergie still was skeptical. Besides, he liked taking the unpopular side in any argument.

"How can you say a million to one, Prof?" he asked. "Is that just some set of odds that you made up in your sleep, or did you really work the problem out?"

The professor stiffened, and it was clear that he was struggling to keep from losing his temper. But just as he was about to say a few sarcastic words to Fergie, something happened. A short, odd-looking man in a derby hat had entered the room, and he approached the display case where the chessmen were. He wore an incredibly dirty and threadbare tweed overcoat, and his long unwashed hair hung down over his collar. His nose was red and bulbous, and half-moon reading glasses were stuck askew on his face. He held a pad and pencil, and as the professor and the boys watched, he began jotting down notes.

Aghast, the professor stared. He made a few strangled sounds in his throat, but nothing came out. Finally he motioned for the boys to come away. Before long they were studying Roman artifacts in another room.

"Who do you think that guy was, Prof?" asked Fergie after they had paused to sit down on a padded bench.

"Some lunatic," snapped the professor. "England is famous for its eccentrics, and he may well be one of the weirder ones!"

"But why was he takin' notes about the chessmen?" asked Johnny in a worried tone. "What's he up to?"

The professor shrugged and looked crabby. "How the dickens would *I* know, John? Sometimes I think that you boys want me to be the world's greatest genius, who can explain the meaning of the universe to you. Look! When I returned the chessmen last week, a lot of reporters were there at the ceremony. The *Times* of London and a lot of other papers covered the event. Probably this guy has been assigned to write some sort of follow-up article. Now, do you suppose we can change the subject? Let's talk about Roman villas in Britain or Boudicca's revolt or *something*!"

Johnny and Fergie shrugged, and they followed the professor to yet another room full of treasures. About half an hour later the three of them stepped out into the columned porch in front of the museum. It was late afternoon, and crowds of people were milling around, snapping photos or just chatting. With a sigh of contentment the professor reached into an inside pocket of his suit coat and took out a black cardboard case that was emblazoned with the Russian eagle. He plucked a black-and-gold Balkan Sobranie cigarette from the box, lit it, and blew a stream of smoke into the air. Now he launched into a boring speech about how polite the British people were and that they should act polite so the British would respect them. Suddenly the professor noticed that the little derby-hatted man had set up shop in the courtyard in front of the museum. He had a wooden folding table with stacks of leaflets on it. As the professor watched, tourists paused in front of the table, examined the leaflets, and bought them. A wooden bowl on the table was full of shillings, sixpences, and even pound notes. The little man seemed very pleased—his leaflets were selling like hotcakes.

With a sudden snort of indignation the professor ground his cigarette under his heel and stalked off toward the table. After giving the man a nasty look he snatched a leaflet from one pile and read the front page.

SECRETS OF THE ANCIENT CHESSMEN

A study of the mysterious ivory chessmen found over a century ago on the Isle of Lewis. Why were they stolen and then returned? Were they originally in the Great Pyramid? Can they be used to unlock the mysteries of Stonehenge? Why have the authorities tried to hide the importance of these occult objects, which may at one time have been buried on Mars—placed there by beings from outer space! Learn the truth as it has been found out by *Murgatroyd Freel, Ph.D.* Can you afford to neglect this earth-shaking book?

For a full minute the professor glared at the table full of leaflets. His face got redder and redder, and he scrunched the paper in his fist. Then he exploded. With a bloodcurdling yell he kicked over the table and wildly threw handfuls of the leaflets in all directions. *"You hornswoggling charlatan!"* he screeched, as the little frightened man backed farther and farther away. *"Get out of here! I'll have the law on you, so help me, I will!"*

As the boys watched, the professor chased the little man toward the gate in the tall iron fence that surrounds the museum's grounds. Near the gate a couple of blue-uniformed guards grabbed the professor and led him, struggling, back into the courtyard. The crowd of tourists, who had enjoyed the spectacle, let out a mighty cheer, and the professor would have tipped his hat if his arms had been free. Instead he smiled weakly and nodded as the guards gave him a severe talking-to. Finally he was released. The officers told him he was not going to be charged with anything as long as he left the museum grounds immediately and did not come back. With a sheepish grin the professor led the boys out into Great Russell Street. They turned left and headed toward their hotel. As they walked along, Fergie could not resist making a comment.

"What was it you said before, Prof?" he asked with an innocent smile. "I mean, that stuff about being polite with the British? I'd like to hear some more about that."

The professor dug his hands into his pockets. "Just zip your lip, Byron!" he grumped. "You should learn to keep quiet until spoken to."

Johnny said nothing, but he silently told himself that this was going to be a very interesting vacation, if they managed to survive it.

JOHN BELLAIRS

is the critically acclaimed, best-selling author of many gothic novels, including *The House with a Clock in Its Walls* trilogy, *The Dark Secret of Weatherend*, *The Lamp from the Warlock's Tomb*, and six previous novels starring Johnny Dixon and Professor Childermass: *The Curse of the Blue Figurine; The Mummy, the Will, and the Crypt; The Spell of the Sorcerer's Skull; The Revenge of the Wizard's Ghost; The Eyes of the Killer Robot*, and *The Trolley to Yesterday*.

A resident of Haverhill, Massachusetts, Mr. Bellairs is currently at work on another thrilling tale.